Swallow the Air

Swallow the Air

tara june winch

UQP

'Cloud Busting' was published in *Best Australian Stories 2005*.

First published 2006 by University of Queensland Press
PO Box 6042, St Lucia, Queensland, 4067, Australia
Reprinted 2007

www.uqp.uq.edu.au

© Tara June Winch 2006

Typeset in 11.5/15pt Bembo by Post Pre-press Group, Brisbane
Printed in Australia by McPherson's Printing Group

Distributed in the USA and Canada by
International Specialized Books Services, Inc.,
5824 N.E. Hassalo Street, Portland, Oregon 97213-3640

Sponsored by the Queensland Office
of Arts and Cultural Development.

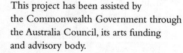

This project has been assisted by
the Commonwealth Government through
the Australia Council, its arts funding
and advisory body.

Cataloguing in Publication Data
National Library of Australia

Winch, Tara June.
Swallow the air.

ISBN 978 0 7022 3521 4.

I. Title.

A823.4

For you
For the words that were whispered
Something mellifluous
For the Moondance
For love
Somewhere distant, silent, gone

Contents

In 1996, Chinese artist Song Dong travelled to the sacred Lhasa River in Tibet to conduct a performance. Song sat in the river for an hour, ritualistically stamping the surface with an old wooden seal carved with the character for water.

Of course the seal left no trace. The impact of the work resides instead with the artist's gesture. Futile and heroic, it recalls those manifest small acts through which an individual attempts to make sense of the world.

And for all of us, attempting to make sense of the world.

Swallow the Air

I remember the day I found out my mother was head sick. She wore worry on her wrists as she tied the remaining piece of elastic to the base of the old ice-cream container. Placing her soft hands under my jaw so as to get a better look at me, Mum's sad emerald eyes bled through her black canvas and tortured willow hair. She had a face that only smiled in photographs. She finished fixing my brother, Billy, also in an ice-cream tub helmet and sent us fishing. Puncturing the fear that magpies would swoop down and peck out the tops of our heads.

She shuffled us out like two jokers in her cards, reminding us to go to Aunty's house before dark, and telling us again that she loved us. The screen door swung back on its rusted, coastal hinges and slammed under the tension. When I looked back down the driveway she was gone.

Billy rode fast, his rod suspended in the distance like a radio antenna. My reel thread over my handlebars – attached with a small bag of bread mix, a flip knife and some extra hooks and sinkers that I'd got from school as a trade for Monopoly money. All was swaying with my slackened momentum.

The sand was stewing. I threw my bike with Billy's below the dunes of spinifex and headed for the point. From there I knew that I'd have the best view of the beach, deep into the surging breakers and practically standing on the locals' surfboards. Last summer I'd seen a turtle from the same spot; he immersed half his body – just to spit. Only a few moments he'd stayed, but it was long enough to remember his beauty.

Mungi was his name, the first turtle ever. They said he was a tribesman who was speared in the neck while protecting himself under a hollowed-out tree. But the ancestor spirit was watching and decided to let him live by reincarnation or something. 'Anyway, using the empty tree trunk as his shell, he was allowed to live peacefully forever as a turtle.' Or so Mum would say. She had some pretty crazy ideas and some pretty strange stories about other worlds and the government and the 'conspiracies'. But the story about Mungi was my favourite. It was what she'd really wanted to say, she wasn't paranoid about a turtle.

I crept over the rock pools; the edges were sharp so you had to walk softly. Gazing down at every shale shape, contorting each footstep onto its smoothness. At the furthest rock pool, searching the ledge for my usual spot, I saw something strange. Draped over the verge was a silvery mould, like a plastic raincoat sleeping on the stone.

Sheltering over the eagled remains, I inhaled its salty flesh burning under the afternoon sky. The stingray's overturned body looked more like a caricature of a ghost than a sleeping raincoat. I stepped back, imagining its tiny frowning mouth screaming in pain. It'd not long been dead and I wondered if it had suffocated in the air or if this was only its mortuary. Either way it had swallowed its struggle.

I pulled it onto the rock ledge by its wing; the leathery shields made a slapping sound at my feet. I wanted someone to see my prize but Billy was way back on the shoreline, too far to hear a girl-ish call. There were three short cuts on either side of its body – where a rib cage would be. They were like fish gills, I guessed, for special breathing underwater. My forefinger slid down its stomach and stinging tail to the tip, tracing around the two thorns that stuck out at the end. In my mind I saw the tail whip across like a garden hose and poison me with a quick and fatal sweep. I sat further away, just to be safe, and thought for a long time about throwing it back in, though I decided it was best kept away from the living, best kept up here in the air.

Pain had boiled up under its swollen body; I could feel the stingray's fight in its last moments of life. It looked exhausted, like a fat man in a tight suit after a greedy meal. But I had pity for the ray; I saw only the release of the dead inside. Stabbing my flip blade through its thick skin, I drew a long gape down the underbelly. An orange sack split open, pierced in the cutting. Oozing paint like liquid, the colour of temple chimes, over its pale torso.

An angel fallen, lying on its back, was now opened to the sky. I was no longer intrigued by cause of death, loss of life. It had died long before I had cut it open, but only blood made dying real. No longer whole and helpless, the stingray was spilling at the sides – it was free.

I took up my bag, blew a loving kiss to what remained and returned to my brother, taking care not to step on the sharp-edged stones.

I remember the beach that day, still scattered with people; the sand had cooled with the falling sun. Blankets with babies and families in those half-domed, tent things. It was that time of the afternoon where mums and dads were getting tired and bodies could get no more bronzed. The entire beach would be packed up in minutes. Billy hadn't caught anything; just a handful of pipis lay in his hat.

'How'd you go, sis?'

I showed him my empty palms. 'You?'

'Just the pipis, maybe we could get Aunty to fry em up, ask her if she got any fish fingers too! Jeez I'm starvin.'

We carried our bikes to the taps and washed our feet. Billy's feet were so much darker than mine; he'd sometimes tease me and call me a 'halfie' and 'coconut'. We'd be laughing and chasing each other around the yard being racist and not even knowing it. I peered out past the bitou bush toward the point, following the pairs of surfers' legs disappearing over each wave. The sea was again a moving silver gull, mirroring sunset's embedded lilac. And I was again a child.

When we arrived at Aunty's house there was a police car parked out front, its wheels scraping against the gutter. There were no flashing lights, no siren. We tossed our bikes into the yard and Aunty leapt off the porch and shuffled us inside, just as Mum had earlier shuffled us out.

Her arms were sticky against my shoulders; she was shaking and sighing like sleeping through a bad dream. She sat us down at the kitchen table and opened the top cupboards, the ones with the barley sugar in them. Though she looked inside at the back walls only to gather her thoughts. She flung her head down, limp at the neck; still gripping the cupboard handles. Aunty cried a lot, it made Billy cry too. I thought she looked like Jesus, with her arms holding the rest of her up like that.

She sounded all broken up, like each word was important but foreign. 'Your mum – she gone.

She gone away for a long time, kids. Me sista, she had to leave us.'

Aunty wasn't sure of the words. They'd never crossed her lips before, not when Mum went to the TAB, not when she went to Woolies either. I knew she was dead.

I took off the ice-cream tub still crowning my head, and stared into its emptiness. Mungi and the stingray floated around in my beating mind. I thought about Mum's pain being freed from her wrists, leaving her body, or what was left. Her soft hands overturned and exhausted. Tears fell into the ice-cream container, dripping off my eyelashes and sliding over my cheeks. Salt water smeared her handwriting of black marker – *remember.*

And I knew it was all right not to forget.

Grab

Aunty never used to reckon she was lucky. She always just figured she was passed a raw deal, dealt a bad hand. I supposed she'd surrendered to being *that* kid, and then to being *that* woman in the same rotting suburb, born into a lifetime of ill fate. Her sister, the only stronghold out of loss, would follow suit in the sequence of lucklessness, and die. Everything, through Aunty's tired eyes, was bad luck. Bad luck until she won the Tip Top Bread Grocery Grab. After the win everything seemed to be a game, a gamble.

It started when Aunty would take the entry forms from the bread stand at Woolies. They never said you had to buy the bread and the checkout ladies never seemed to mind. Every pension day she set aside five dollars for stamps, and then she'd trace her name in thick memorised letters across the forms that still smelt of cooked flour. I don't think she really believed she would actually win anything; maybe it had been her time to at least try.

I wasn't there when she went to Woolies that pension day. Aunty told us when she saw her name up on the big poster she had to pinch her arm to make sure she wasn't just dreaming. She came home and told us how great Christmas was going to be. *We're gunna have a bloody Christmas turkey this year, my loves.*

Billy and me stood behind the barricades of streamers with Tip Top Bread balloons strung from our hands, a crowd of the other contestants' families engulfed us at the front of the supermarket. Aunty had three minutes to fill her trolleys with anything from the aisles of labels. Her fingers wrapped tight over the trolley handle, light brown knuckles pushed over from the grip. The timer began to count down. 5, 4, 3, 2, 1, Go! She flung her wobbling hips down the first aisle whilst Billy and me chorused the names of all the chips and lollies that we had scabbed from the other kids at school, stopping mid scream to piss ourselves laughing.

Aunty was piling in arm-sized cans of beetroot

and pineapple slices. The one-minute timer was counting, 5, 4, 3 . . . We saw her start to panic and skip a bunch of aisles, targeting the trolley towards the frozen food section. You could see on her face the dread, thinking any second all time would be up. She got caught there in the frozen aisle, throwing in white plastic-wrapped turkeys and frozen chickens and pastry pies. The trolleys filled faster and faster, their hospital castors wobbling under each load. The presenter ran up to the far end of the supermarket where Aunty was and began flinging empty trolleys up the aisle with one hand, a microphone attached to a long black cord in the other. The trolleys sat stray and bloated, swollen like fresh driftwood. By the time the fire engine lights and the shrill siren flashed and shrieked through the supermarket she had three full trolleys, two of frozen food. Exhausted, she wheeled the last trolley, slower now, back to the checkouts for a quick interview, puffing and laughing.

Aunty leant over the barricades to Billy and me to give us a big hug, clapping her hands together and laughing. *We don't even own a bloody freezer!* She half whispered it at us and we looked at each other laughing. Aunty asked Billy to count how much was in her purse: fifty dollars. We each took a trolley and craned their heavy baskets to the taxi rank outside.

'Can you take us to the hockshop, please, driver? Take us to the best one and there's a turkey with your name on it.'

He looked back at Aunty with night-shift eyes and a toothless, thin-lipped grin, as though a Stanley knife had just slit open the skin between his fat nose and the end of his chin. He sped the station wagon to a second-hand goods place just down the road and stopped right on the footpath. Aunty asked him to wait with us and she came out a minute later, the sun spiking the shine of the white rectangular freezer being wheeled out by the salesman. Big jolly smile still on her face.

I remember that smile, we mirrored it, and I reckon it was the happiest day of her life. She was at last lucky. From the front seat in the cab, she looked back at us and said it herself. *I think kids that I'd have to be one of the luckiest people around!*

She laughed at her luck then, and all that Christmas, right up until the food ran out and the vacant insides of the freezer iced over. It stuck to her though, that luck, like a scrounging leech.

It was the scratchies at first, four-dollar winners were pinned up against the fridge, while tens of the losing stubs lined the bins. Then it was lotto, then trifectas, pool comps and then that slapping death knell, the pokies. We rarely saw Aunty those days, when we did, she'd just lie about winning, or where she'd been. Aunty drowned out, she faded from our safety.

I try to imagine what she would've been thinking, perched up on a bar stool, tapping at the plastic, lit-up buttons. Raising the stakes. Hoping to light up another grocery grab or that fortnight's rent money or the electricity bill with Paid ink-stamped across it. I suppose that when those clinking dollars chimed in the shiny metal gutter, all those bills and red-letter promises disappeared. And it was just another bonus, another incentive, a quiet celebration for her luck.

Another drink.

Cloud Busting

We go cloud busting, Billy and me, down at the beach, belly up to the big sky. We make rainbows that pour out from our heads, squinting our eyes into the gathering. Fairy flossed pincushion clouds explode. We hold each other's hand; squeeze really hard to build up the biggest brightest rainbow and Bang! Shoot it up to the sky, bursting cloud suds that scatter, escaping into the air alive.

We toss our bodies off the eelgrass-covered dunes and race down to the shore where sea-weed beads trace the waterline. Little bronze teardrops – we bust them too. Bubble-wrapped pennies.

We collect pipis, squirming our heels into the shallow water, digging deeper under the sandy foam. Reaching down for our prize, we find lantern shells, cockles, and sometimes periwinkles, bleached white. We snatch them up, filling our pockets. We find shark egg capsules like dried out leather corkscrews and cuttlebones and sand snail skeletons, and branches, petrified to stone. We find sherbet-coloured coral clumps, sponge tentacles and sea mats, and bluebottles – we bust them with a stick. We find weed ringlet doll wigs and strings of brown pearls; I wear them as bracelets. We get drunk on the salt air and laughter. We dance, wiggling our bottoms from the dunes' height. We crash into the surf, we swim, we dive, and we tumble. We empty our lungs and weigh ourselves cross-legged to the seabed. There we have tea parties underwater. Quickly, before we swim up for mouthfuls of air.

I'm not scared of the ocean, that doesn't come until later. When we're kids we have no fear, it gets sucked out in the rips. We swim with the current, like breeding turtles and hidden jellyfish, as we drift out onto the shore.

We climb the dunes again, covered in sticky sand and sea gifts. We ride home and string up dry sea urchins at our window. We break open our pipis and Mum places each half under the grill or fries them in the saucepan, with onion and tomatoes. We empty our pockets and line the seashells along the windowsill. Mum starts on about the saucepans; she wants to tell us stories even though we know most of them off by heart, over and over, every detail. The saucepans, she says, the best bloody saucepans.

Billy and me sit at the window, watching Mum while she fries and begins. I'm still busting clouds through the kitchen pane, as they pass over the roof guttering and burst quietly in my rainbow.

'It was Goulburn, 1967,' Mum would begin.

'Where's that?' we'd say.

'Somewhere far away, a Goulburn that doesn't exist anymore,' she'd answer and carry on with her story.

★

Anyway, Goulburn, '67. All my brothers and sisters had been put into missions by then, except Fred who went and lived with my mother's sister. And me, I was with my mother, probably cos my skin's real dark, see – but that's another story, you don't need to know that. So old Mum and me were sent to Goulburn from the river, to live in these little flats. Tiny things, flatettes or something.

Mum was working for a real nice family, at the house cooking and cleaning; they were so nice to Mum. I would go to work with her, used to sit outside and play and wait for her to finish.

When we came home Mum would throw her feet up on the balcony rail, roll off her stockings and smoke her cigarettes in the sun. Maybe chat with the other women, but most of them were messed up, climbing those walls, trying to forget. It wasn't a good time for the women, losing their children.

Anyway, all the women folk were sitting up there this hot afternoon when down on the path arrived this white man, all suited up. Mum called down to him, I don't know why, she didn't know him. I remember she said, 'Hey there, mister, what you got there?'

A box was tucked under his arm. He looked up at us all and smiled. He come dashing up the stairwell and out onto our balcony. I think he would've been the only white person to ever step up there. He was smooth. 'Good afternoon to you', ladies, I am carrying in this box, the best saucepans in the land.'

Mum drew back on her cigarette and stubbed it out in the tin. 'Give us a look then.'

The suit opened up the box and arranged the saucepans on the balcony, the sun making the steel shine and twinkle. They were magical. All the women whooped and whooed. The saucepans really were perfect. Five different size pans and a Dutch oven, for cakes. Strong, black, grooved handles on the sides and the lids, the real deal.

'How much?' Mum said, getting straight to the point.

The suit started up then on his big speech: Rena Ware, 18/10, only the best, and this and that, lifetime guarantee, all that sort of stuff.

The women started laughing. They knew what the punch line was going to be, nothing that they could afford, ever. Their laughter cascaded over the balcony rails as they followed each other back into the shade of their rooms.

'Steady on there, Alice, you got a little one to feed there too!' they said, seeing Mum entranced, watching his mouth move and the sun bouncing off the pans.

He told her the price, something ridiculous, and Mum didn't even flinch. She lit up another fag, puffed away. I think he was surprised, maybe relieved she didn't throw him out. He rounded up his speech and Mum just sat there as he packed up the saucepans.

'You not gunna let me buy em then?' Mum said, blowing smoke over our heads.

'Would you like to, Miss?'

'Of course I bloody do, wouldna sat here waiting for you to finish if I didn't!'

Mum told him then that she couldn't afford it, but she wanted them. So they made a deal. Samuel, the travelling salesman, would come by once a month, when money would come from the family, and take a payment each time.

Mum worked extra hours from then on, sometimes taking home the ironing, hoping to get a little more from the lady of the house. And she did, just enough. And Samuel would come round and chat with Mum and the other ladies and bring sweets for me. He and Mum would be chatting and drinking tea in the lounge until it got dark outside. They were friends after all that time.

Three years and seven months it took her. When Samuel came round on his last visit, with a box under his arm, just like the first time, Mum smiled big. He came into the flat and placed the box on the kitchen bench.

'Open it,' he said to Mum, and smiled down at me and winked.

Mum pressed her hands down the sides of her uniform then folded open the flaps and lifted out each saucepan, weighing it in her hands, squinting over at Samuel, puzzled. With each lid she pulled off, her tears gathered and fell.

'What is it, what is it?' I was saying as I pulled a chair up against the bench and could see then in one pan was a big leg of meat, under another lid potatoes and carrots, a shiny chopping knife, then a bunch of eggs, then bread. And in the Dutch oven, a wonky looking steamed pudding. Mum was crying too much to laugh at the cake.

'I haven't got a hand for baking yet. Hope you don't mind I tested it out.'

Mum just shook her head; she couldn't say a word and Samuel understood. He put on his smart hat, tilting the brim at Mum, and as he left the doorway, he said, 'Good day to you, Alice. Good day, young lady.'

And when Mum passed, she gave the pots to me.

★

When our mother finished her story she'd be crying too, tiny streams down her cheekbones. I knew she would hock everything we'd ever own, except the only thing that mattered, five size-ranged saucepans, with Dutch oven. Still in their hard case, only a few handles chipped.

I run my fingertips over fingerprints now, over years, generations. They haven't changed much; they still smell of friendship. I suppose that to my nanna, Samuel was much like a cloud buster. Letting in the sun, some hope, the rainbow had been their friendship. And I suppose that to Mum, Samuel was someone who she wanted to be around, like a blue sky. For Samuel, my mum and Nanna, I don't know, maybe the exchange *was* even, and maybe when those clouds burst open, he got to feel the rain. A cleansing rain, and maybe that was enough.

My Bleeding Palm

Billy got a job on the milk run and Aunty got pissed to celebrate. It felt like everything was a celebration then: when I got the year-eight art prize at school, when Aunty had a good day on the pokies, when we had Chinese food. It seemed just about anything called for celebration. With Aunty there, every night was toasted. We were happy when Aunty was happy, laughing and yarning and dancing around the yard. She'd be flat on the grass and still dancing in her head, eyes glazed with an absence, a bliss. I imagined her as an angel, laying out her wings beneath the satellites of the sky. There she soared.

I could gaze out on that backyard for hours, patterning circles in the grass, like a cat ready to pounce. Sunsets were for staring at across the long sweep of disorder, over rooftops where the day would snigger and slowly hide its semi-circle of tangerine.

'I'm goin out, ya kids be good for ya aunnie, right?'

'Yeah, Aunty,' Billy called from the fridge door, 'we be good.'

From the back steps I watched the loose heel of her stiletto drag along the hall carpet and disappear through the door frame, like an arm that's been slept on all night, all paralysed at the bend. Aunty was off again to see her boyfriend or whatever she confessed him to be. I followed an invisible line back from where she'd stumbled from the mirrored basin. Where she'd drawn cocksucker red lipstick over her black lips in worship of her prince.

Aunty got a boyfriend. Skin just like mine. I'd hear Aunty cry all the time. Fists of black hair. Cheek to the stove. Don't know when my real Aunty is gunna come home.

'I'm goin for a walk, Billy, back soon.'

'Yeah, watcha back for the boogie man!'

Billy grunted in his thin belly before filling it with a bong. I slipped through the broken palings that the council were supposed to fix years ago, a splinter hiding its shard between my forefinger and thumb. Behind me I could hear Billy pop the cone and cough on his heartache, lunging back unlove.

Paradise Parade, built over the old Paradise Abattoir, bore two long rows of housing commission flats, unregistered cars, busted prams and echoes of broken dreams, all crammed into our own special section of Woonona Beach. Paradise, ha! Way down, past the flags and half a million dollar beachfronts, there hid a little slice of scum. From the wrong side of the creek, we'd had the privilege of savouring the last crumbs of beachfront property. Soon they'd demolish all the fibro and move us mob out to the western suburbs. For now we were to be satisfied with the elitist postcode and our anonymity.

The cycleway was the only thing that bound us to the estate properties that bred rapidly from the dozed clay beds. Big terracotta storage boxes. *Here is my wife and these are my children and this is Bingo the dog, oh, and let me show you the patio.*

The liquorice ocean blew its chilly Pacific spray against my presence, each quivered lip caught in the undercurrent of a quarter moon. She drew back her sea's crown and swallowed my fear. We were like the morning ladies, doing tai chi: out with the black clouds, in with the white. Clean.

I squinted through the darkened clouds, eyeing the serpentine cement path. Out of sight the sounds syncopated with the tide, like a basketball bounced against a car bonnet – the compressing of air and the jolt of metal. I drew behind a bottlebrush bush and pulled back a fresh branch, bending on bracket knees, trying to get a glance. The hard glow of suburbia cast patterns of destitute light on the openness. Nothing. The sounds twisted louder over my ears and through it I heard someone scream. The lads were out. I strained to see what was happening.

I once knew the cycleway well. Billy and me would ride this way to Bellambi Beach when we were kids, when the nor-easterly currents would get rounded into the southern bend of the beach. There, at the mouth of the creek we'd find blue swimmer crabs for cooking up. Only certain times of the year you could find the crabs though, all the months with the letter *r* in them Mum used to say. It wasn't often too that the channel would be opened up to the beach and as we got older we began to feel like we didn't belong on that side of the creek either. Trailing behind the graffiti tags strewn among the grey. '*Mull up lads . . . fuck off coons.*'

I began to hide my skin from the other beach, from this stretch of cycleway. There were bends all through this part, I remembered. They wouldn't see me, I thought. I'd run along the side of the path and hide in the dune entrance further up near the creek. *Ready set . . . Keep your knees bent, don't look, hear the voices, keep low, not far, not far, quiet, here it is . . .* down.

'See that man, some little friggin spyin broad . . . *SEE THAT*!'

I watched him tilt with his shadow. He was alone, still against the light crashing on hurling bodies. His mates were too busy taking apart one of the kids – probably one of the dope runners ripped them off. Payback, slamming his rag doll body between the Datsun panel and Nike.

I hid deep in the scrub and tried to see through the condensation of screams. The line of white press-studs that ran down the side of his tracksuit caught the moonlight as each leg strode toward the walkway. I slid under the dune fencing and doubled myself into the pandanus branches. I am invisible, I am earth, I am sand.

'Oy, ya little coon bitch, what tha fuck do ya think ya doin?'

The bottle dropped to his side, dribbling onto the sand. My eyes flickered at his slippery face, his fat bottom lip tucked under his front teeth, sliding off, sucking the dregs of beer, drawing a ball of spit, glaring sliver-eyed at my slightness.

I scrambled up and ran toward the water; my feet cupped the dunes and spat the damp sand sideways, my arms flailing the whipping southerly. The panting of terror drew behind me as my shirt gave way and dumped me over, heavy kneecaps, hands and sand tormenting. We're down, we're stopped, and a blade caresses my cheek like a sympathetic breeze.

'This gunna show ya where ya don't belong dumb black bitch.'

The popping buttons over my back take me elsewhere. Bubble wrap. Lemonade burps as Billy and me push each plastic blister between finger and thumb, choking on each other's laughter. Popping giggles silence violent grunts.

He ends it mutely and clips back his buttons: pop ... pop ... pop. I forget to feel the blade swim through my palm, shallow, seeping blood.

I do not nourish, I do not even turn over, not even when he leaves, this be my death, where I quietly finger the softness of my tongue.

Bushfire

From the head of the escarpment, I used to think that I could see the world. When I was younger, when Mum was still here, I'd ride up to the quarry or the old miners' trails, always with secrets. I'd push through the thick scrub faces, where in the ferns I'd hide. And the ferns would hide too, or try to. Their feather prongs always peeking through burnt-out car remains and the o-rings of washing machines.

It was always wet up there, always a cloudy place in the mountains. The middling trees would gather last night's sea breeze in their canopy, away from the sun, letting cold dewdrops fall on passers-by and soft winds. Slicking sweaty skin and sleeking hair strands against my face.

That summer, just after Mum left, the fires started. Every year they got worse. It stopped being so wet, the dampness fell away from the soil, and up until Christmas the whole coast would shift into a furnace of dry salt and smoke.

The year I was fourteen the bushfires would not be packed away in manholes and hall cupboards with the Christmas tinsel; they stayed on right through January and into school's first term. The nor-easterlies drove the red ginger skies to the wall of the coast road, and soon the entire national park that kept outer Sydney from our coastal town was left a charred break-wall, a warring deaf-black distance.

On the news it showed birds falling from the skies; they'd hit the pillows of smoke and drop to the earth like little soft bombs. Ash dropped from the sky too. All over Wollongong fragile cinder flakes stained hung out linen and car bonnets and drifted into the southerly swell. The ocean kept the sooty snow afloat and at night the smoke kept the fires lit up, so that day and night blended into each other, so that everything appeared both carbon black and hazy yellow or a constant humming orange.

At the end of January a postcard arrived, redirected from our old house down the road, to Aunty's. It lay in the shade of the flip top metal letterbox, the handwriting side showing, addressed to us Gibsons, our family name. *Sorry it's been a long time.*

Sorry.

The postcard was late, too late for Mum. The ink had been wet before, its dotted *i*'s and stroked *t*'s seeped across the boundary. *From Dad*, from Dad.

Sorry.

From Dad.

I walked my bike out from the side gate, slid my hand into the letterbox and tucked the post-card into the side of my shorts, so that the glossy cardboard stuck to my fleshy hip. And then ped-alled as fast as the heat would let me to the quarry, at the base of the escarpment.

At the entrance to the miners' track, beside the strangling figs and purple lantana, I left my bike and headed up by foot. The ground was dry, as it had been for so long. The track was swept with a thick cover of brittle, banana-shaped leaves from the gums, and sunburnt palm spines, that criss-crossed their way up the sloping dirt. The smell of fire still rose, even from so far away; it belonged here with the other odours of dust and mining and sweet banksia blossoms.

In the small clearing, where I'd hide shaded by umbrellas of grass trees and tree ferns I took the softest ground as a seat. It was dry there too. When it was damp and you'd sit up there for a while, you'd be sure to find a leech on one of your ankles or sucking the blood from between your toes. Mum used to say that these parts are famous for their leeches, or used to be anyway. She said that the old people used to trade them, big juicy fat ones, they'd use for medicine. She said that the people from this part are called the Dtharawahl people, and dtharawahl means valley, a perfect wet breeding ground for leeches. It is their land, Mum would say, so we have to help look after it for them in exchange for our staying here. Be respectful, she'd say.

But there were no leeches anymore; they left when Mum left – traded for the bushfire's arrival. Maybe they were hiding deep in the soil where it was still a bit wet, waiting for the rain to come and moisten the hard crust, waiting for the rain to make mud so they could slither out for food. I imagined all the other animals that survived the fires would've been hiding too, waiting for the right time to come out and start again.

Maybe Dad had done the same. Maybe he needed to hide away until now, until he could come back. I wondered if he'd come back.

Sorry it's been a long time that you haven't heard from your old man. I'm up here near Darwin picking mangoes on the harvest. The season is over soon and one of the blokes here's going pearlin out west so might send you some treasure. From Dad.

The shiny photograph on the postcard was of a pretty display, a pile of orange mangoes, strawberry hibiscus framing them. There was another photo next to the first, of palms between rows of huge thick-crested trees, which leaked their branches into the slender grasses below. Against one of the trees was a ladder; a canvas picking bag was slung off a rung where a man was standing. It wasn't Dad; the man had a big wad of blonde hair and was clutching a mango, as if to pick it.

I didn't know it then, but the man would no longer be there and the mangoes would've all been packed and sent away in dusty oversized trucks. They would all be bought and eaten, the skin and seed rotted, the yellow dew leather chewed through by worms. Fruit flies would have flown to new flesh. And the dark finger leaves would've grown over in pink wax scale, the hibiscus turned black and the sweating fragrance of caustic sap and sugar long been buried with the season.

But to me, then, under the thick mangle of brown branches that pleaded for rain in the desperate dry air, he might as well have been right there. He could just as well be perched on the other side of the escarpment, or down at our old house. I'm five years old and we're eating powdery watermelon, spitting black pips with a mouthful of giggles. Or I'm about six, following his forearms, his fingers as he shows us how to cast the hand line off the beach, swinging the hook and sinker, his aim perfect. How to pull up the slack of the nylon line, gently. His arms are strong and pale, I remember, as I follow them out to the breakers. Watching the bream and whiting surf the waves in huge schools like dolphins. Before the line would take and he'd reel in a catch. I'm six still and I'm watching his bare limbs heaving a shovel in the backyard, the sound of the blade hitting the damp clay, the smell of the exposed soil, weekend cut grass and his sweaty back moving like the tide. I can still see his fingers moving unconsciously as they roll a smoke, flicking the lighter and drawing back on the cigarette. The muddled smells of White Ox tobacco and yellow Palmolive Gold soap on his hands.

He might as well have never left. I wondered how I could ever have thought he did, how I could've allowed the memory of my father to pass me by, to cease existing.

And the memories all came back then, bit by bit, shiny little bubbles, quick, sharp. Just before they spit open and disappear again, clear.

Leaving Paradise

No one taught Billy how to fight. Mum had once said to me that he just had to; he already knew before he was born that he had no other choice. His heart was bleeding before the world had even got to him, before he could even swallow air, Mum had said.

She was just a young girl when her stomach started to swell like the full moon had gone and grown itself inside her. She was just a young girl when the doctors said that her little baby might die. That they would have to cut open his chest and patch the holes in his heart, that afterwards he might not live very long either. That little brown baby had two setbacks then, she thought.

Billy's dad ran away, he was the right skin for Mum too, but he wanted to play rock'n'roll instead, wanted to live in a swag or the back of a Kingswood, no place for a sick baby and a young mum.

A year later she found out that he had driven up to the Blue Mountains, outside of Sydney, that he'd rented a cabin at one of the villages along the ridge. That he'd woken one morning, the type of morning where clouds hustled into the side of the mountains, embedding themselves thick in the pines. Letting each indent of the valley be filled with mist, those mornings where everything seems silent, a faint echo of a car or birdsong somewhere far off and empty. That he'd walked out to a lookout and jumped straight through the fog and into the sandstone base of a waterfall. That something must've been itching him bad.

But Mum still thought that boys needed their dads, needed to have men around to grow into. So she went and found herself another dad for Billy, a white fella. And a few years later I arrived. But Billy was still sick, he'd turn yellow soon as you looked away, dropping off, fainting, his heart too slow, or too fast. Those doctors never really did get it right. The stitching came away like loose shoelaces and his heart would be bleeding again, leaking inside his skinny little body.

When Billy could finally stand though, he refused to sit down. Mum knew then that he'd be ok no matter what happened, that he was a fighter in his heart, even if it was his heart that was barely fighting.

★

One day at the beach when we were kids, I remember running my finger down the melted ridge of skin between his ribs. I asked him if it hurt but he said he couldn't remember. The scar felt slippery, I remember that. And then we never talked about it again. I never thought about it again either.

Not until the day Billy turned eighteen.

We were still there living with Aunty, though mostly she was either out or out of it. The booze had got a strong hold of her, her and her boyfriend Craig, and the bottle was what the house turned into, not a home any more than she had meant for it to be. Just a place of grog and fists. Craig had a rage, I hated him for hitting her. I asked Aunty why we didn't just go, but Aunty said he'd never remember the fights, that he'd have blackouts – and that he couldn't help it. Poor Aunty.

Every night it happened, I began to wake

before they'd even come home, my body waiting for the back door to fling open and bang against the wall, for them to be already at each other's throat, or laughing and chatting before a blue would start. I'd lie awake through the whole thing, my breathing so loud that I was sure that if they'd stop bashing into each other for a second, that through the walls they'd be able to hear the air passing fast and heavy in my throat.

But they didn't stop, they'd keep going until they were exhausted and one would plead with the other to have a drink, would say sorry and drag em to bed.

Night in and night out, on the other side of the walls that held our Aunty and some stranger captive: two puppets of booze trialled their messy, confused violence. But this night, it was Billy's eighteenth birthday and it'd be the last fight either of us would hear.

That afternoon Aunty had given Billy a silver flask. We sat around the kitchen table with a sponge cake and candles that I'd bought from the Vietnamese bakery. Singing happy birthday, the three of us, Craig in the lounge room. Aunty, sitting there smoking and sipping a cuppa, told Billy to jump up and grab the blue plastic bag near the washing powder in the laundry. We giggled while Billy made this dumb look on his face with a bit of a smile as he went out to the laundry.

He came back to the kitchen with the bag and untied the crumpled, bow-eared handles at the top. He didn't drink grog but Aunty said it's a keepsake anyway. Billy liked it. She jumped up and grabbed it off him. 'Here ya,' she said spinning the lid off the bourbon bottle and holding the flask over the sink. 'Fill it up for when ya wanna have a drink one day, on your wedding night, boy!'

Billy's face went all red and he pulled a cheeky smile at his feet. She tightened the flask and grabbing the tea towel off the bench, smudged the case clean.

'There!' she boasted. 'Your mum'd be so proud of you, the both of you.'

Billy and I dropped our heads down. Aunty was gettin all tipsy and emotional. I didn't mind her like this so much.

'Garn, get out. Go meet ya mates.' Aunty scoffed him off with the back of her hand and threw herself in front of the TV.

'Ya wanna come?'

'*Me*?' I said.

'Course, you dickhead – what are bros for?'

'Where we going?' Big smile crept across my face.

'Movies – my treat, but we're watchin *Terminator*, ya reckon ya can handle that?'

'Yeah *yeah*!' I said, stirring.

At the cinemas Billy's mate Vardy and him went halves in my ticket. I was so stoked. I remember walking into the movie thinking, *yeah this is my brother, the best brother in the world*.

After the movie we decided to walk home. Vardy started drinking the bourbon from Billy's flask. Then Billy drank some too. They took big gulpfuls and winced. Billy and Vardy started getting drunk and raving about the movie.

They would take turns at saying 'I'll be back' in the Terminator's voice, jumping over front fences, tripping into people's yards, falling over wheelie bins and pot plants before running back to the footpath for us all to piss ourselves laughing. They'd take a swig, pass the flask to me then run into the distance.

I was laughing so much that I thought I'd have

a swig too, a little tight-lipped sip so that only a tiny bit passed my lips. I'd smelt it before, but the taste was bitter and antiseptic. My head whooshed dizzy and I belly laughed at the boys more and more with each sip.

It was so much fun. We said seeya to Vardy at the bottom of Paradise Parade and as we walked the street, he and Billy flung *I'll be back*'s over front yards and fence lines until we got to Aunty's, laughing our heads off still.

We cleared the back steps and into the kitchen. It was quiet except for the low murmur of Craig's voice and Aunty's faint whimpers. He had her black hair all tangled in his thick fingers fist, the red metal coil of the stove plate a few inches from her face.

It happened so fast. We'd never stepped between them. Billy pulled back Craig's arm, grabbing at its thickness. 'Let her go, ya mongrel!'

Craig's fist freed itself from Aunty's head, flinging her downwards. His arm rose and hammered into Billy's chest. The thud was bottomless, booming against the stale kitchen.

That's when I remembered.

As Billy's mouth opened wide and sucked in

air from the pit of his stomach, his eyes dilated. He brought his open palm to his chest – the place where his heart lay beneath the skin. He tumbled backwards onto the linoleum, a dead weight.

The kitchen light swung slowly back and forth across his body. Billy's eyes were wide and searching the ceiling. My head whooshed more, I dizzied above him, too shocked to touch his weakness. Billy's hand was still against his chest as he grabbed Aunty's eyes with his own. His scream was from somewhere deep within. He bellowed, baring his teeth, yelling miles and miles of hatred upon her. It seemed like forever that the sound pelted out of him and up to her face.

He pushed himself off the floor and charged to the fibro wall, kicking his foot through the chalky plasterboard as we all looked on disbelieving.

'Fuck this place, fuck you all! Fuck this shithole of a house, fuck this town, and fuck this life. Let's go May, ya comin? Fuck this for a home. I'm not comin back, May. Not ever. Let's go.'

He stood at the back doorway, his chest heaving adrenalin. My head fogged over, the alcohol no longer giggly, it shivered inside me, suffocating any normal judgement.

'Let's go, May!'

Again and again he threw the words at my hands, hands incapable of taking hold of them and running. I could only stand and sway as he punched his fist into the back door and disappeared into the night. His screaming flung through the streets like *I'll be back*'s, but I knew he wouldn't.

When I walked up and down Paradise Parade, to Vardy's house, to the beach, away from the chaos of Aunty and Craig, away from everything we hated, as I walked the empty black streets, I realised Billy was really gone.

Billy and me were like shadows; we could merge into the walls without being noticed. We'd move on the same tides; when we were laughing we couldn't stop each other, when we were talking neither of us could get a word in, when we were fishing, being sad, or being silent, we were both empty cups. We were rarely angry, we rarely fought, and if we did it was only if I was annoying him, and even then he'd just chase me and kick me up the bum and it'd turn into us laughing together again.

We didn't talk about Mum or our dads or all

the booze and shit around us, we knew the world in the same way that we knew each other, in the quietness that we shared. It wasn't in our eyes, or our voices or what we said, it was just there, that understanding, that sameness – it slicked our pores, our skin. It was a feeling that you couldn't see, or smell or hear or touch; you only knew.

I thought I'd know where he'd be, up the bush, at Bulli Beach, thought I could track him down, thought he'd be where I'd go, the same. But I looked for days, weeks, months. He never came back to Aunty's, never for clothes or for a feed or to find me. He'd really gone.

And the more he wasn't there, the more I realised too, we were all gone.

To Run

Sometimes people stand in the way of other people's eyes. I wasn't waiting for change; I wasn't waiting anymore for things to get better. I took the mango into my mouth, my teeth traced in yellow stringy sweetness. I took all of him, away from Aunty, away from her fermented eyes.

She didn't see the postcard from my dad like I did, she couldn't see the piece of me, even if it was only paper. She held her booze like a butcher's knife, cleaving off each part of herself – and her own. I would sit on the back steps, blocking out her drunkenness, only imagining Darwin. *If you could be any fruit what would you be?* I would be the mango that breaks off the stem into my dad's fingers, the apple of his eye before I slide into the picking bag.

★

I pulled the zipper of my backpack tight over the nylon. When it reached the end of two rows of teeth it busted open and a slight gap of black shine hung out like a sock end. I stepped off the porch and padded across the grass to the cycleway, feeling like a seagull, taking the air into my wings, tucking under the busted red leg that wouldn't matter in flight.

I knew a squat where a friend had been staying; I'd been there with her once to pick up her sleeping bag. I remembered they said I could come round. The words stuck to me. 'Come back and stay anytime, sister.' The invitation shone beyond the damp memory of the house, through its empty lines, the wet walls.

The house wheezed, jammed between the new motorway and the train line, alongside the lapping sidewalk that rose and fell like undulating limbs. The garden path ran through the small yard where a woman and a man were arguing, her hand gripped his pawpaw bicep as she grunted into his face, muttering something about money. I traced around them, to the steps and peeped through the open door.

'Hey, girl! I know you don't I? Who *are* you?

He sits cross-legged in the sunroom beside the frayed vinyl lounge. 'You've been here before, I know you!'

His hands closed in his lap fly out and grab memory from the space between us.

'Yeah, I've been here; I'm looking for my friend Crystal. She was stayin here, hey?'

I thought back to the time I'd visited, there were people hanging around everywhere, a drug house of anxious nobodies. And now, here I was, hiding that same, quiet desperation.

'Yeah yeah *yeah*, Crystal, she's a nice girl, haven't seen her for *ages.*'

I watch his eyes move from the thought of Crystal to my rucksack. 'Need somewhere to stay, girl?'

'Yeah . . . Last time I was here, you guys said I . . .'

Before I could finish, he'd jumped up and was leading me down the hallway to a big room with a drum kit and a mattress in it. He grabbed a piece of foam off the mattress and laid it down in the opposite corner.

'Welcome. This is my room but I don't mind sharing. Don't worry, it's safe.'

He went on about how he got his name and

where he was from and the rules of the house; *community* he kept saying, shooting thoughts like tearing open birthday cards. I could hardly track his jagged mind. He was friendly and kind of jittery and silly with a mange of tight curly hair, like a jack in the box or, as some must have thought, a sheep.

Sheepa gnashed his sentences a few times and broke into a grin, his jaw quivering under his top row of teeth like scared magnets. 'Anyway,' he began to exit back down the hallway, then turned and leapt at me gently, 'you like poppies?'

I followed him to the rotting kitchen, I held onto the door frame, to half hide fear. I trusted him. Should I? I didn't care anymore. It didn't matter.

In the kitchen Sheepa rinsed an old cola bottle clear. From under the sink he took a plastic shopping bag and emptied half the little black dots into the cola bottle and filled it again from the tap. The water pipes shuddered under institutional cream walls. He shook the bottle for a while, tilting back his head and looking into my face, calmer and more real than before.

'What's it do?' I asked.

'It'll take the hurt out of your eyes.'

I brushed my fingers across my face as if turning diary pages, smearing secrets along my skin, owning them. Before I closed the book and looked away.

Sheepa tightened a sock over the top of the bottle and strained the muddy water into a glass. The grey water didn't dazzle or twinkle in any midday light; it sat as dull as my heart. Launched by his blunt chewed fingers it slid towards me across the flecked bench. I took the glass carefully to my chest and walked back into the room. As I sat against the edge of the foam and let each mouthful bleed down my insides, every nerve ending and muscle lay down its guard. And soon I felt less confused than before.

★

I am lying on a bed of foam, though my skin knows it as water; it rises to my pores and laps at my ear cavities, muffling the choke of intersecting roads, of voices, of wind. Belly up to the sky where whitewashed clouds let out the blue like venetian blinds. The warmth swims up around my neck and outlines the painlessness of my face, of me. And from here I am perfectly happy. From here I stay, unwiring this bliss behind eyelids that make pictures and movies. I dream I dream I dream.

In the movies I am there, I know it is me but my face is blurry, and the other people in the movies I know too, but they are also blurry. My cousins are there and my dad too, we're inside the house looking out into the yard where he's chasing a blue tongue around with a shovel. He's jumping and heaving the metal rusted blade into the sandstone and dead garden beds. He's angry, but we're laughing at him. Then he turns towards us, his eyes come into focus and he's crying, but he can't help it. There's blood spitting down one of his legs. He comes up to the window, and now instead of the shovel he's resting on the lawn-mower handles, the motor's running still and the noise drives me back to the room, I'm halfway between and he's still crying. I can't stop him from crying. He leans down and pulls a beer bottle top from the flesh of his shin. He's laughing hysterically, as if the possibility of the event is so small, as small as a beer bottle top.

The movie changes and I'm swimming, I'm

always swimming, and Mum is swimming too. We're diving through salted waves, catching our breath, before we realise we needn't breathe. I look toward her but she's not there anymore. And when I open my eyes again I'm in the middle of three lakes, a gutter runs through the centre where I wade. Where I stand feeds the lakes, the shore, the mango tree in the distance, the black cockatoo circling my head. A lone grey kangaroo drinks at the water's edge. When I imagine he is there, when I believe he is there, he looks up at me and stretches back, resting on his tail, displaying all that grey muscle, flesh and fur.

I wake. Again and again.

When I feel trapped walking in my head, solving unsolvable mysteries, I drown, and the releasing surges out of me, pungent flowing vomit, freeing. The drug doesn't recognise me anymore, doesn't recognise that I even exist under its hold.

I witness more spooling movies. Dad has come and gone, as he did. Or would have. I think about when he left, I can't remember why, it torments me; it keeps me awake for days trying to remember. I feel this kind of frenzied serving dish in my belly; it fires and burns with an aching for my father. There has been fighting, for how long I don't know, it's always just there, in my mind. I ask my brother if he remembers, or if it even matters, but his face is blurred and his mouth has not yet formed. I wonder if I am beginning to understand things, or if I am losing grip, like Mum.

Sheepa entered the room. He gave me two pink notes, his shout for lunch, but I must go to get it. I don't enjoy crossing the busy road to the corner store. Inside, my skin begins to grease, the frying vents seem clogged up and a thick yellow blanket rests at the ceiling. The stench of oily potato and stale fish fills the small shopfront nook. The red-haired woman square-dances around the fryers, dipping a metal basket in and out of the swampy liquid. While her back is turned, I pocket a packet of noodles and a Mars bar. I think she knows, but she needs us and we need her. I promise myself I'll stop stealing, when I'm old enough for Centrelink.

She glares over her glasses at me.

'Two hamburgers with the lot, thanks.'

I walk outside and dump my body in the chair on the footpath, my back melting into the hot plastic. Even with the bushfires finished, the Gong is still a fighting city. Smoke from the steelworks competes with the hot air that clings brown orange to the coastline, the haze that has filled my lungs since my first breath at the hospital, the haze that has hung over the backyard of Paradise Parade and singed the dim, glittery nights. To the west, the escarpment traps the grubby air, keeping it from escaping still; the shop's clogged vents work in the same way. I let the warm plastic cradle me, imagining some huge clean openings in the sky that would suck all the shit out. With the heat, you choke on it – you taste the dirt.

I stare at the fragile clouds and loosen my thoughts before my eyes drop focus on the house. And just then my heart fell into the pit of my body, bruising its hard shell. All feeling jolted back into me as two men and a woman enter the house. One is Billy.

How long had it been? I counted a few months as I balanced on the median strip, waiting for the traffic to speed past. I skipped past the tail of a car and into the sunroom as fast as my smile had leapt onto my face. And left. Just as fast.

'Billy! Where have you been?'

'Hey!' He turned to the others. 'This is me little sis,' he slurred, drugged, and staggered into me, throwing his weak arm around my neck. 'May baby,' he started to hum a tune. '*May baby.*'

I wriggled from his smelly chest and rested against the doorless frame in the hallway entrance. I tried to catch a glimpse of him, but he wasn't there.

'You're off ya dial, Billy!'

He was humming to himself and shaking his head, a song and a joke carrying on without anyone else. As his hands unwrapped the small package of foil, the others waited to shoot up. Their eyes were all sunken brown and yellow stones, cold. Golf balls bending earth colours, the mud from their veins and lungs and heart spreading what they felt over what they saw, insides had become the outsides and hope was suspended, just beyond view.

I went back to Sheepa's room unnoticed, with more than a door separating us. Placed all my little things together, rearranging them. Little pretty things – a black cockatoo's feather; the postcard of mangoes from Darwin, my pocketknife and a tiny tray of blue shimmer eye shadow.

I rearranged the little things again and dreamed.

Voices drowned under poppies, where everything was slow and smiley.

★

I woke with the fear of brown and yellow eyes and dragged dead legs to the bathroom to check. A girl was there, I'd never seen her before. She was slumped on the floor. Her clothes fell from her as though shedding themselves in the heat. She was wilting in a puddle of peach-tiled water, a little pool of sweat gathered at her naked hip, where the name '2pac' was inscribed in green. She was beautiful.

A little river of foam left the edge of her lips where she spoke.

Blue roses

Burnt

She had no eyes.

'Please, Sheepa, come here.' I squashed his face together and ground my teeth. '*Pleeeeaase!*'

He dove up as if thrust out of nightmare, the others followed. In the bathroom he ran the shower cold and dumped her melting body into the bathtub. She had no eyes. She did not wake. He slapped her white cheek firmly but gently. It remained white. She had no eyes. She did not wake. I stepped back helpless as they dragged her dead-weighted, almost corpse out through the sunroom and down the steps. Billy was holding her legs. He glanced up at me as he shuffled backwards. He was vacant. He had eyes. He did not wake.

I followed them down the path, past the blurring traffic and to the train station stairs. I'm confused. I have eyes, no mouth.

They disposed of her like evidence and the train took the blank girl along the lines and away from the empty platform. Sleepless sleepers.

I did not know any of them; I did not know my brother.

Back at the house I placed the little pretty things in my bag. I waited at the edge of the new motorway, in the stirring exhaust pillows, waiting to go to wherever.

Territory

The truckie was heading straight to the Supercharge Raceway in Darwin. Melbourne to the Top End. He said he never usually went the coast road, but the bushfires were spread out west and this was the only way. He said that from here onwards there'd be less traffic, he said it to reassure me, but I didn't mind either way. He'd been there before, Darwin; it was where he'd met his missus. He told me about it as we drove. Diving in and out of his stories of the raceway and of a sweating community that dangles on the edge of the Arafura Sea.

A big country town, Pete said. His arms grabbed the top of the steering wheel as he arched his back, stretching. 'Yep, nice people and good pubs, and good fishing of course.'

★

To see the ocean disappearing in the long passenger mirrors, seeing the wide blue ribs of the coast fall away beneath the ridge, let me finally breathe. I thought about us putting the girl on the train, her slumped body, out of it. I wondered if she was dead, if she'd ever wake from that sleep among the sleepers, or dream a life away.

I wondered if Billy ever would too. I wanted to forget him, his dead eyes looking through me as he shuffled the girl away, shuffling himself further from me.

On the motorway cars had rushed by me faster than ever until finally a truck dropped its gears as it passed me and waited, rumbling, further up the stretch. I ran up to the passenger side where Pete had flung open the door and smiled. Not a creepy smile at all, a fat teddy bear smile full of metal-filled cavities that made me feel safe.

In the back of the truck there were three Supercharge cars, which were to be raced that weekend. Pete said then he'd like to just rest his voice box for a while, he liked to drive in silence, said he's got four kids at home and it had been a long while since he'd had time to think, said if I didn't mind, could we just listen to music and mind our own beeswax. I told him I'd like that too, and I did.

Day eventually gave way to night, where the road and the sky faded into a mask of sparklers, scattering stars and headlight scars across the hours. We drove right through Pete's box set of country classics, and his energy drinks, right into the third repeat where I began to memorise the lyrics.

He wanted to get there by tomorrow arvo, for the fights before the races. Said it'd make it the best weekend of his life if we got there on time, said he needed to keep awake. As we passed through the long stretch from the sugar cane fields to the wheat stalks, he took the little bag of white and with his bank card against the logbook crushed it out so that it was smooth. He lined it up in skinny rows, sucked each line up his nose and grunted his way through to daylight. I lay half asleep in the cab's bunk bed, as suspension collapsed over pockets of repaired tar, counting his mutterings.

A memory slipped in between the sheets and me. Dad is there. We're at the side of our old house. He's crouching beside Mum's racer with a spanner;

he's tightening the bolts on the wheel rims. With one hand he holds the bike frame above the cement and with the other spins the wheel round. The red and blue buttons slide up and down the spokes. He looks over to me, smiles.

Perfect.

★

By the time I opened my eyes against the day; the sunrise had already shifted above the top of the cab. My muscles ached, as my bones stabbed against them with the truck's sway. I felt crook, my insides abandoned, like a hulled out apple. Just the skin to cry through, little tears welled at my pores. It was the poppies. Opium sweats, Sheepa called it, the morning after a night without them. He would boil up a pot of pineapple juice, cook it so it was warm and add some spumante to knock that shit feeling out of us. Opium bones, muscle ache and nausea. If I could make it through this, I knew I wouldn't miss that feeling again. If I could make it through.

'Mornin,' Pete said through his mercury teeth that matched his earlobe full of metal rings. His hands still rounding the steering wheel, his eyes fixed back on the moving road, the same looking road as yesterday. The only difference was maybe the dust, embracing the road a few shades redder. Heading towards the blushing Top End.

Pete said there wasn't long to go. A quick feed stop and we should be there by the arvo. He shouted me baked beans, fried eggs and bacon and a cup of hot coffee, for the road. The grease slipped out the edges of my lips before I caught it with my tongue. Meals like these could either cure the pain or feed it. I waited.

The day disappeared again in half-sleep and twanging banjos from the speakers. I asked if I could turn the sound down a bit. He said it was fine; he was getting sick of it anyway. He didn't take his eyes off my hand and forearm as I reached out for the stereo.

'You got really olive skin? Ya parents, are they European or something?'

'Na.'

'What then? Ya got something. My missus, she's Maltese. Skin like yours too.'

'My Mum was Aboriginal.'

'No shit? You don't look like an Abo.'

'My old man isn't though; his family are from the First Fleet and everything. Rich folk they were, fancy folk from England.'

'I hate Pommies,' Pete said, and back in the music and the silence, I wondered if they really were from England after all.

I couldn't wait to find Dad and ask.

*

Pete points at the little green shields on the side of the highway, they have a number and a letter or two above the number. He says that sign will tell me how far away we are from where we're going. The next one that I spot has the letter D and a 98 written underneath. 'How long does that take?'

'Depends if there's any towns to go through matey, but probably around an hour and a bit I reckon. But we're going to take a detour, a pit stop, kid. Local attraction – only Fridays, won't see it again. You'll love it…'

And soon the highway forks and we drop gears onto a skinnier road that leaves the white paint outline behind. We drive a fair while down where the trees have begun to overgrow the crumbly bitumen edges. I almost start to panic until the side of the road opens up to a field of parked four-wheel-drive utes and troop carriers. A hand-painted sign dangles from the back of a tin shed. Palm Creek Rodeo.

The truck's gears take their final dropdown, hissing and shuddering the cab, as Pete drives over to the end of the field and stops. We climb out onto the steps and fling ourselves down.

We begin to walk across the jumbled rows of cars, when the sun falls just below the tree line and a cool wind catches my nape. I loosen my jumper from where it's tied around my waist.

Pete's pink skin is camouflaged among the sea of red dirt cars as we near the side of the shed. A big wind pushes its way beneath the four-wheel-drives and beckons at my legs. The boundary of eucalypt trees cry out above clawing desert oaks, as they perch themselves on the land. A big gust flings the trees backward and then forward like the concave of lungs. The air whooshes about the trucks and whistles deep in my ears, I throw my head up to the sky's bellowing.

Grey gums inhale. Pausing breath. A slow thudding noise replaces the sky; it drives over the rodeo fence as I pull the jumper over my head, the hood crowning my face.

What I saw was not meant for my eyes.

A jawbone crunches under a slice of bare knuckles. Bloodied eyeballs throw blank expressions. Mouths fling spittle streamers about the dirt red ring. Frantic, finger-bitten punches claw tangled in the shiny skin.

I hear Pete's voice in my head, *the fights before the races.* I can't take my eyes from the horror, the osmosis of blood and blood beneath the dust-flung dusk. Bones crack under the fighter's grated ribs, his oars of the dinghy swinging – slipping to the ground. The fighter thrusts a knee in between the other fighter's lung cage. It caves him skyward like a skinny stray cat. All the men roar back. Fierce men. Black men and white men, separated by only skin, only by skin until it rips open and the red blood and red dirt become the same, same red brute. The smell chokes me, fighting, of Aunty's Tooheys Old, unwashed sheets, marinated, raw beef. The fighter who's down, half naked and pissing his pants and pleading, is taken under the armpits and dragged from the ring, leaving the short ditch of urine and blood across the ground.

And as another fighter clears the fence, I notice the money-shuffling hands. The stink of bourbon leaks across the fifty-odd men and the few bleached heads of tattooed women. Leaking from belly laughter and sing-along heaving breath.

I wrench my eyes from the blood, and up to the faces, the spectators, not like I'd imagined rodeo men, more hard shiny faces and no cream creased shirts. They wear big hats though, guilty of some principled crime underneath their wide brims.

★

Some things you never *ever* forget. The way your dead mother used to smile. The way sunrise flashes against the tabletop of the ocean. My brother's scared eyes looking up from the kitchen floor.

Some things stay with you, even if you manage to prise them out of your history, they somehow come marching back with a slung shotgun to blow away anything you've managed to build. To destroy your world, the world that's not real but you wish it was.

And I'll never ever forget that day, at the rodeo

fights, and all the days that that day had brought with it. The day that I found my father. There he was, watching the men bleed faces. There he was, Dad. The day I truly faced him, at his side, not the stranger I'd wished for, or made myself imagine. He was the monster I'd tried to hide.

He had a hand like a claw, so full of engorged veins and leather red welted skin, so strong and like his face that hung mirroring the ravaged. How could I forget him? His fingers slung over the cigarette as he sucked from his lips that were pressed close against his forefinger and thumb. His neck contorted against the inhaling charred breath. He hunched over the whole habitual scene like he always had, down at the flame and across the room. That look, that exact face. That was his anger face.

I remembered now, when that anger face became his always face and the world ceased to be real, to be able to be understood, so I had left it behind. I couldn't remember the endings to the memories of him. But here they were laid bare – the bores of him that I had hidden. Exposed for the fluid truth to punch through.

He is there. We are at the side of our old house.

He's crouching beside Mum's racer with a spanner; he's tightening the bolts on the wheel rims. In one hand he holds the bike frame above the cement and with the other spins the wheel round, where the red and blue buttons slide up and down the spokes. He looks over to me, smiles, because he hears the car pulling into the driveway. 'Stay here and play,' he says as he rounds the corner to the back of the house. Through the walls I hear the spanner; it thuds against a void, and then shatters the bathroom tiling, that chiming noise. And it's just a mess of skin now, slapping and slow pounding. 'You fucking bitch.'

Midnight whimpers, so faint, so light as if never of a victim. We see it through the crack of our bedroom door. Billy and me, watching Mum's head swinging into the cupboards, her crazy hair flinging into her own bloody mess. 'Don't tell me to get a fuckin job.'

He's run out of yarndi, he heads inside the house, clearing the back steps. We hide in the corn stalks that Mum had planted. We don't huddle together, Billy and me – we are separated by the violence.

Mum is in the shower. I can see him in the

kitchen; he's boiling the kettle. I see the steam rise as he rips the jug cord from the wall and disappears into the hallway. This time she screams. His aim was always perfect, like sunsets.

And Mum could grow her hair see, leave it out and let it go crazy. Let it hide melting skin. It's a shame women are so clumsy. Let her hair go crazy, like they thought she was, crazy just like he had made her.

I remember now, my mother was a beaten person. She wouldn't scream at his fist, she wasn't the type to fight his torments. She bottled all the years too; until one day all those silent screams and tears came at once. And with such force that they took her away. The screams must have been so deafening, the river of tears so overflowing that the current could only steal her. The flood breaking so high, that she had to leave us behind. We couldn't swim either.

Mum's stories changed when he left. She became paranoid and frightened of a world that existed only in her head. Who was going to beat her mind? Dad wasn't there anymore, but she still saw him, he still managed to haunt her. I remember the madness, the fear. Was he hiding under the bed, Mum? Was he in the cupboards reaching out for your wrist? Was he under the house? Is that why you dug up the backyard? Why you became blank and told us nightmares instead of dreamings?

Poor Mum.

And now, I could let him go. Because only when I remembered, could I finally forget.

I tugged on the drawstring of my hood and walked back to the truck. I waited until Pete threw himself up into the cab and rocked with the suspension.

'Bit outta control there, hey? Only in Darwin, bare-knuckle fights. Only in the Territory! Don't worry; you'll never see that again. So, where to in Darwin, which resort are you staying at my lady?'

'I'll get out on the highway; I'll be right on the highway, Pete. Gotta go back, I forgot something.'

The Block

I'm in Sydney, in a pagoda sipping Japanese tea or a castle where I wait for a carriage made of baked pumpkin to take me from here to anywhere but here. I had pumpkin soup at a street kitchen yesterday but the taste was shit. I could do with a feed, a good feed. Sleep was fine, but that free food was a load of rubbish, no one ate there unless they were real desperate. It's a weird neon place forever decorated as Christmas, a forgotten stretch of Pitt Street stone.

I'd headed south that day, I remember, in the passenger seat of the backpackers' station wagon, the foreign voices dousing the sunset colours of the Top End. The shiny bits of the car sparkling red like all the blood I'd ever seen or imagined. It was then that I knew Pete was right. I knew that I would never see anything like that again.

The trip ended in the middle of this mad city.

I arrived with my heart still hurting and my head still spinning. I realised I hadn't cried at all since I'd left Wollongong. My eyes began to harden like honeycomb. It got easier to do, being tuff.

I spun into the clogging traffic and muffled voices and tides of ironed pleats and searched for the nearest tree. These buildings were like a bed of sprouted nails; I dragged my fingers across them, smooth granite, marble, mirror glass, sandstone and pebble. Around and beyond the still life, for miles, was a crawling, prickly blanket of identical houses and roads.

In the middle of the chaos I found Belmore Park, directly opposite the station. Lining its bitumen streams were massive fig trees with strong muscled roots that cradled strangers and split open the otherwise faultless lawn.

In the centre of the park, through the scattered yellow-brown maples, is a little brick house, a hexagon with a parachute cover of mouldy tiles as the roof. The sign reads Belmore Park Depot, but people call it all sorts of names – the pagoda, the gazebo, or the first floor. I'd rather think of it as a castle, when you're up there you feel as if you're sleeping under the stars on the battlements, a balmy night in some fairytale village in a cartoon, with its fancy steel stake fence that wraps around the rooftop. But the cartoons don't scream and ambulances don't ribbon the streets clean of its spilling blood, drunken businessmen don't get rolled and the gangs from Chinatown don't come to do deals. The cartoons have bullshit happy endings to make people hope, for a prince or a hero to save us from whatever it is, the dragon or the robber.

I didn't need to be saved; I wasn't waiting for a stupid hero.

But one came anyway, not in a costume, but wearing a purple t-shirt, and baring too-perfect false teeth.

'Hey, *moguls*, ya little cunts, ya up there aren't yas?'

I was awake already, lying on my side watching the branches dance. I propped myself on my elbows at the sound of her voice and dragged my belly to the fence to look over the edge. An old woman with white hair neatly combed and parted stood staring up at me.

'Little sis, who are you?'

'May Gibson.'

'Any young fellas been round ere?'

'Nah, haven't seen any.'

'Well whatcha doin up ere anyway, May Gibson? Get down ere and talk to ya aunty girl, what ya doin sleepin round ere, bloody *moguls* ere.'

I threw my leg over the metal stake and slid down backwards, wondering what a *mogul* was. 'Just needed somewhere to stay,' I said, looking at the ground.

'Well don't be shame now, everyone need somewhere to stay. Some people got it and some doesn't. Come stay with the women and me. Beats being around bloody strangers, you got family in the city too girl, come have a feed.'

I nodded, remembering the shit pumpkin soup, and climbed back onto the ledge to pull down the blankets and my bag. The old woman was already walking across the park, I ran up beside her. We walked fast across to the station. The city seemed to become softer behind us, quiet, as if we were the only people in the place.

At Central I went to the toilet and washed my

face, holding my head under the dryers, feeling the wetness swim to my hairline and disappear. I looked into the mirror. *You got family in the city too girl, gunna show ya where ya don't belong dumb black bitch, you don't look like an Abo.* The words swam in my ears. When I looked into the mirror I saw a girl, lost and hollow – the same as every other fifteen-year-old, I guessed. I didn't see the colour that everyone else saw, some saw different shades – black, and brown, white. I saw me, May Gibson with one eye a little bigger than the other. I felt Aboriginal because Mum had made me proud to be, told me I got magic and courage from Gundyarri, the spirit man. It was then I felt Aboriginal, I felt like I belonged, but when Mum left, I stopped *being* Aboriginal. I stopped feeling like I belonged. Anywhere.

We got the train, only one stop. As we stepped onto the platform she told me I was to call her Joyce, if I needed to find her ask for old Joy. 'Just stay with us women and ya be all right, little sissy.'

Joyce coiled her thin fingers over my wrist and walked me faster up the steps and across the bridge. The place was heaving with people, people walking with groceries and prams and kids, people boozing, people laughing, people being. The walls of the bridge were covered in massive paintings of black faces and flags painted to look as if they were flying high in the sky. We walked through another park, much smaller than Belmore, without trees, nothing except a couple of dead-looking cabbage palms in the middle of a circle of pavers. A wall followed the railway lines covered in more huge paintings. The houses were tall and narrow and as we swept down past a row of them I noticed they made a kind of square, like the walls of a box. People started to call out, yelling Joyce's name and asking who I was. Joyce just kept walking, leading me by the wrist.

The door was opened; Joyce led me through and shut the door behind us, clamping the handle with a chair.

'Sit down, sit down,' she pulled out a cushioned crate from under the table.

The house was small. Paint flecked the cement walls crumbling around photo frames. So many faces. Joyce put the pot of water on the stove and looked back over her shoulder at me and then to the wall of people. 'This is my family,' she said admiringly and started to point at the smiles, ' . . . my daughter Justine and my other daughter, she's dead though and . . . '

She dissected the whole puzzle, taking a few frames off as she spoke and wiping the inside of her shirt on their glass covers, second cousins and great grand kids and aunties and mother's brother's uncles.

'We're all family here, all blacks, here, from different places, but we're all one mob, this place here . . . '

She pulled back the dirty lace curtain; we looked out onto the cement and tar.

The terraces colliding into each other. Rubble edging fences. Rubbish clogging gutters. Mothers screaming fathers or brothers or cousins. Uncles drinking, thinking under bread and butter. People giving their whole dole to the bowl that is empty, that they turn right over as if they got plenty. Drug smuggling thugs the mothers. Baby cries for others. Fits uncrucify the losers. The grinning winners looking down from two towers. Metal rods flog *moguls* on the grog. And they're spitting and spinning out. And some places don't sleep, only drown.

'This here a meeting place for our people, always. Welcome to the Block, little sis.'

That was my first contact, the rest just got more confusing but easier, until I just became immune to it all. Growing up in the bloody Gong was nothing compared to a year living in the Block. I went in like a buttery cake and came out like a shotgun or a Monaro or a gaol sentence. Came out like a steel wall adorned in black tar.

I stayed with old Joyce most of the time, her and her daughter Justine and Justine's boy Johnny. They were my family, and I loved them.

Most nights at Number 7 Caroline Street Joyce and the other aunties would stay up yarning and playing card games like jackpot and drinking sweet wine until all hours of the morning, around the same time when the bonfire in the park would start to whimper, and sirens would be sunk out with the silence. I loved staying up with the women and just listening, chain smoking and sipping hot sugar tea all night.

In the day Joyce and I would talk between us. She'd tell me all about growing up on the Block, about how her nanna had come and taken her back to Sydney when she was only little, a bit younger than me. She came here and worked in Wilson's paper factory, making notebooks and writing pads. She laughs about it now, stretching back the loose skin over her porcelains and pointing across the street at the flat ground. 'Just there,' she says, as if she can still see it with her own eyes, as if she can still smell the watery bleach and warm, smokey fibre of the paper, 'that's the old factory.'

She told me about the history of Redfern, about the housing corporation stealing everyone's money and homes, about how it used to be a real strong community. 'And now,' she says shaking her head, '*it's the young fellas taking our money as well and the drugs stealing our community.*'

Joyce said the place was broken most of the time, but sometimes, mainly Sundays, it was beautiful.

I grew to love Sundays too, dry days when the flat ground turned into a churchyard and most people smiled big.

★

When you start to not feel the punch that lands on her face, when you begin to see someone's broken heart instead of someone's bruised veins, when you know that cuz needs a beating to sort him out, you begin to see love more than hate, that real sort of love, the sort that's desperate and always fighting. Fighting to be heard and stay.

Joyce always made sure I was inside by dark, always made sure I had a feed. I wanted to buy food too so Joyce helped me get a job. Her cousin's missus' brother used to work at a carwash and he told Joyce that they'd give me a job. Shit money but it was cash in hand so it was good for the business see. I did end up getting the job, for a while anyway.

Things seemed to be going good, but sometimes Joyce would put the hard word on me, after she'd had a couple of sherries and all the aunties had gone home. And the bullet would always drop somewhere in the middle of my ribcage.

She was packing up the cards one night when she cornered me about my family. 'So . . .' she said with a caring prying tongue, 'where's all your family, girl?'

'After Mum died, we went and stayed at Aunty's and Billy, well he–'

She interrupted with a jabbing finger, her jet eyes bolting ya face. 'I know all that, May, what about your nannas? You got old dobs in yer mob like me?' She straightened up against the table, making herself look taller and tipping back her head all prided. 'Go on, what about ya old girl, her mob, where they?'

'Dunno, she left us so long ago, I remember stories though and I know she's Wiradjuri – from out west isn't it, Joyce?'

'*Wiradjuri!* You *Wiradjuri* blood girl? Well all ya mob's probably out ere in the park drinkin.'

She bellowed laughter across the walls and glass-covered faces. They smiled back.

'Yeah, yeah,' I said, forgetting where I was.

She caught me.

'Ninganaa little one, have some respect.'

She was serious.

'Now listen good,' she said, pulling out a crate again. 'I know ya like it ere, but it's no good ere little one. You know what I'm talkin bout, no good young dobs growin up in this ere, and I'm gettin too old to be worryin all the time bout ya, specially after that carwash business the other day . . . I know, I know you got ya young sissy girls ere and Johnny, but you, May, you got people that you gotta find, things you gotta learn. You *will* learn them ere, but I don't want you to. Look at Justine, smack the only thing teachin her now! You gotta go, May, you got sumthin to find, fire in the belly that ya gotta know. See all the *moguls* now, they got the fire too, but people in the city always gunna try put it out, then it outta control. You know, like trying to put the fire out with petrol. It ain't workin. Not while government puttin fear on us.'

She took another mouthful of sherry. 'Think about it, May Gibson. Who they Gibson mob anyway? They gotta be somewhere out there.'

I felt shamed, like she didn't want me there anymore. I pulled a loose thread from the arm-chair's doily, unravelling its sticky string shapes. I sat there silent until Joyce packed up the cards, took her sherry by the neck and went upstairs. The lights flicked off the staircase and the house was dark.

Sadness crept over my hands, over my body and for the first time in Sydney I cried. I cried floods that washed down to the city quay and filled that dirty harbour. I cried all the way to Waterloo, I cried the hoarding off old terraces. I cried with the rest of us.

Chocolate

Railway lines like fragile taping rose and fell through the scarce green. I searched my fingers, sleepers of cracked wet flesh-folds like bleeding nectarine seeds. I checked myself in the reflection as we passed under tunnels, pressing the collars of my Cheapa Petrol polo shirt, looking down at my chemical hands cradling that big watermelon.

Charlie and I would take fruit every day for smoko, sometimes a bag of oranges, or a pineapple. Sometimes Charlie would even bring a punnet of strawberries and we'd sit in the sunshine at the entrance of the carwash and juice each red berry, staining our lips. And always after we'd finish our ritual he'd roll a thumb size of lime-soaked tobacco and line his gums for the rest of the day, vacuuming Mercedes and chewing down the copper muck. On the sunny days

Charlie would get out his piano and play it cross legged inside the perspex walls. 'For good sound,' he'd say, stopping mid-tune and pointing to the roof. 'Good sound, hey!'

I'd nod and be taken away again by the beautiful music. Charlie called it an *mbira* or a special thumb piano; it was a block of wood with shiny metal teeth that he flicked up and down with his long thumbnails. I'd close my eyes and see a velvet jewellery box with a pretty ballerina pirouetting against the mirror. The dinging tunes dancing her along.

'Yes, sir, yes, boss, I'll do that boss, right away boss. Sorry boss.'

Mr Tzuilakis would seesaw between the car-wash and the office. In the indecision he'd walk back into his cramped cardboard office, as Charlie would gather up the instrument, make some tobacco juice in his mouth and spit down onto the cement behind him. We'd watch Mr Tzuilakis waddle out at least twenty times during the day to check on how well we were cleaning the wheel caps or this or that. He'd sort of strut around, looking at you while he counted the sponges, two sponges per bucket. If a sponge went missing he'd always yell at Charlie. Looking right down his finger pointing, into Charlie's glare. '*You watch it hah! Just watch yourself, boy.*'

But Charlie was hardly a boy; at fifty-four he still worked harder and faster than every employee at Cheapa Petrol – the console operators, Jan the office lady, me, and even Mr Tzuilakis himself. I imagined Charlie as a chief or a hunter and back in Africa I suppose he was.

He'd never tell you about Africa, and I never asked. It was his secret – his past, that someday, revisited, would become his home again. He never asked me where I was from either – it was an unspoken understanding. We just existed there in that carwash, carwashers, crouching with fruit nectar dripping off our chins. Spitting the sour blood onto the cement.

That day, I'd brought watermelon.

'Hey, trouble! What you got there?'

'Watermelon, ninety-nine cents a kilo.'

His smile poured out like curdled milk and brown theatre curtains. And it was then I thought Charlie could have been my father, or wished he was secretly, looking up for his approval, hoping he'd lean over against my forehead with his and tell me softly, as if I'd known all along, that I was his child.

'Hey, Chocolate,' yelled Mr Tzuilakis.

Time lay itself down over the acre of grey. Bowsers drank the air and all those shuffling, smoking cars just paused, with their owners, for however long forever is. A police officer walked over with Mr Tzuilakis, another lagging behind with hands on hips as if each of his strong index fingers and thumbs were lifting and placing mechanical legs. I noticed the legs of all three men's trousers, perfectly ironed, each mechanical leg. Then they leant over and without words stole Charlie's smile.

They waltzed him to a car like dance partners, lowering him under the doorframe to make sure he didn't bump his head. They took turns to shake Mr Tzuilakis' fat hand and then lowered their own selves into the car, and drove away past the stack of firelighters and the cage of gas bottles.

Chocolate rang in my ears; I thought it was funny that Mr Tzuilakis called Charlie by the name Chocolate or Boy, never Charlie. *Charlie and the Chocolate Factory.* Just like the movie. It was really funny. I thought about that until

Mr Tzuilakis walked over and said I ought to get to work, pack up the hand wash. 'Can't hand wash just one of you.'

I thought about it while he explained what the word 'deported' meant.

I thought about it until he waddled back in.

I thought about those blue suits taking away the people I love. The cops at Aunty's house that day and now Charlie. I hid back in the chemical room and got out Charlie's thumb piano, flicking its teeth a little, numb and confused. When I went back out to the auto washer a couple of fellas were hanging around the side, in the garden.

'Hey, sista, nice shirt.'

'Whata ya want?'

'Just doin some shoppin ya know, sissy, got any stuff we can look at, ya know some cans there, sissy?'

Silver and pink paint flecked their upper lips, bottles hiding under their shirts. Chroming was common, second to drinking and yarndi but first choice to petrol. It was always easier to steal a few spray cans than fill a jerry of petty or risk getting chased out of a bottle shop by some meathead.

'Nah, piss off I'll lose me job, everything's counted.'

'Yeah all right, reckon you can give us a jerry then?'

'Ya gunna pay or just do a runner?'

'Nah we pay, sister.' He shows the end of a ten-dollar note from his pocket. 'Ok, sister?'

'All right,' and pushes the note back in.

I go into the service station. I walk the chip aisles checking the new jerries a couple of times; some new young guy working the console ignores me, slipping fingers through a magazine and gulping a Coke. I grab the jerry acting all-casual, and walk toward the automatic doors.

'Hey, carwash girl – where are you going with that petrol can?'

'Just a customer, out at the wash. Don't worry, once he fills it up I'll bring the money in.'

'Yeah all right, don't forget.' He rolls his eyes blindly across the packed-out bowsers and back down at the mag.

I walk out to the bowsers and fill the can to the top. Screw the lid on tight and walk over behind the muddy perspex walls. The fellas aren't in the garden and the chemical room door is flung open,

I walk over and stick my head in on them.

'Whata ya think ya doing?'

Before they have a chance to answer or run, Mr Tzuilakis is standing at the entrance of the carwash, his hands on his hips.

'What are *you* doing miss?'

'Mr Tzuilakis, oh um nothing just . . .'

The fellas step out of the doorway and run out the side, a big bottle of tyre cleaner in each of their arms. Mr Tzuilakis just yells out to them, too big to move. He looks over at the jerry can and me. 'Your friends are they? Well it's not the first time I've had to call the police twice in one day.'

'No – please, boss, can't you just sack me instead?'

'Don't worry, May, I'll be doing that too.'

Mr Tzuilakis shakes his head down at me and strides back to the office. I move fast, grab Charlie's thumb piano and the watermelon and run to the traino, dodging the main road through warehouse yards.

I jump the train to Redfern and wait in the park for the police car to leave Joyce's house. They'd already come for me.

I sneak around the side and through the

window. Joyce catches me as I flop through onto the floor.

'Joyce, please, you have to believe me – I didn't flog anything.'

'I don't have to believe ya, May, I do though.' She widens her eyes at me. 'They racists down there anyway, I've already called Tzuilakis on Shelly's phone, told him he could stick his fuckin three dollar award wage bullshit. May, May, May, don't know about all this trouble girl, we'll talk later.' She reaches out and presses the collar of my shirt with her thin fingers. 'We could unpick that logo you know, not a bad shirt, May.'

'Yeah,' I say.

She strains the murky white water from the pasta in the sink, talking out the back window to me.

'Yep, I'll fix it up for ya girl. Go on then, clean up, lunch is almost ready.'

'What is it?' I say, trying to round the edges.

'A feed, May, it's a feed. Go wash up.'

Wantok

Johnny takes me away, together we run the white-sanded beaches, and we eat mangoes and pick coconuts and wade through swamps to pull up lily roots and eat them as sugar rhubarb. Even if we're sitting there in Caroline Street or walking up Vine to the park, we've escaped with each other and the rest of it – the Block and the city rise up and drift away like vacant echoes.

We follow the train tracks to Central, we rake in the city and buy hot chip rolls with gravy, we go west and discover streets that even Johnny didn't know existed; there we play hockey games with wooden stakes and beer cans. Johnny says it's not the same as in Waiben but it's still fun. In Waiben he says they use tree branches and they carve their own balls from wood. He says Waiben is his real home, where his father lives.

We talk of the beaches and our old folk, them and something missing.

Johnny Smith was born four months before me; we worked it out, exactly to the day. He was born in Sydney though, not Waiben. He hasn't been to Waiben yet, but he knows that it is his home. Johnny said he was going to get initiated, but Justine was in lock up so she couldn't come to mourn the spirits. He reckons he's still going to go up and get cut. He says people call it Thursday Island, cos Thursday is pension day see, the best day of the week, and that's why they call it that, cos it's so good up there that everyday is just like pension day.

When I first came to Joyce's he'd tried to crack onto me. I remember us sitting in his room at Joyce's, him blowing bong smoke through the gap of the window. The way he looked at me, it was nice, a gentle look, but I told him to piss off, told him all men are bastards.

'You're my girlfriend, hey? Me and you?'

'Piss off. All men are bastards. Don't reckon you're any exception!'

'Nah, girl, you've just heard that from TV and stuff, magazines've brainwashed ya. That ain't true. Look at me – I'm no bastard!'

'I *know* all men are bastards. Even if you're not, even if you're just too young to be a bastard – don't worry you will be one day.'

We stir each other up, joking. We know we are just best friends.

He always tells me about when his uncles have travelled through the Block, come and stayed with Joyce even. She'd make them a big pasta feed and they'd tell him all about the Torres Strait. He told me the same stories.

He says in the islands lots of people live in houses on high stilts, perched up in the leaves of pawpaw trees and towering black palms. He says that you can reach out from your window and pick off a ripe mango. Just like that.

He takes my hand like always and we scramble up the palms and hack down coconuts with a machete, we run down to the rocky beaches and cast off our canoe, we fish all day, following the reefs and tides and winds. We read the ocean looking for dugong, we beachcomb for turtle. We visit the other islands and trade food and sing songs. We dance with palm branches and deri flowers, like we are spirit people. We rest in the houses as warm tropical storms light up the bruised sky. We lie out on the high balconies and watch the ocean turn to ink. Osprey hawks soar in from the deep, they plummet feet first into the stirring water, when they hit it they fold their wings downward and lift up into the air, a fish slipping in their claws. They return home, like us, to nests. Their nests are like houses, stacked high above the water line atop rock outcrops in the hot billowing wind. We rest.

In the late evening when we wake, I take *his* hand and lead him to my mum's country, to the lake. We wade through the delicate water, the moon spilling on our colourless bodies. Brolgas ruffling their wings against water ribbons, making the muddy bath flinch in coiling waves. We dig hollows in the wet sand and become snakes, silting though the swampy streams, creating mouths and rivers. We make fires, hunt red kangaroo and wrap ourselves in the warm skin and sand. We sleep.

We run back to Joyce's house, and hang out on the little veranda. Johnny's cousins come round and we listen to music under the sunshine. Daylight blanching our dreamings, the gritty air fuming back to our noses, engines starting back in our listening, and we remember what we're all really seeing. Beach lines of gutters, trunks of layered windows, metal wings fleeing the sky, and dinner on the stove. We don't mind, because anytime we can leave in our minds.

It isn't bad when we come back; we notice little similarities to our dreaming places. The cabbage palms, the fire pit, the family.

I suppose that's what makes it, family, and I suppose we don't see the faces in our dreams yet. We promise each other to find them, the faces, to go to our homelands for our people, for ourselves. We are best friends. Johnny says I am his *wantok*, his black girl ally. I tell him that he reminds me of my brother. And he says he is my brother, always.

Painted Dreaming

Staleness oozed from the pores of plasterboard, yellow, blue and fluorescent green spilling along the symbols, words, along identity. I went and hung out with some of the streeties. The old Waterloo terrace had been our canvas, our outlet. Etching ownership out of aerosol. The falling of colour cured us. It wasn't the existing but the enduring that I needed. All of us did.

One-step forward, two-steps back, no home again. Fifth time that fortnight that the pigs came to clear us out. Living, making camp, was no right of ours. From one chipboard door to another, inviting themselves in as if enacting a progressive dinner, searching for signs of surviving. Some of us leapt out of windows like high jump horses; spray cans spun on their sides like break-dancers. They shot paint into the officer's face, his eyes bleeding his blindness. Savages. The paddy wagon cage let in the city air, thick and stifling and real.

We submitted names and far away homes. Undressed. They gave us tracksuits; the brown fleece caressed my limbs. The watch-house roof fell on me like a marble domino. Small chrome sink in the corner: toilet and washbasin. Two metal bunk beds stuck out of render like forklift trays. Symmetrical bars framed the dark place where train tracks met. I drew the government-issue, cactus blanket over my face and dreamt of places, away from winter and walls.

Windradyne was angry. There was betrayal. There was war. Sharp spears through thick skin. He rose from the rivers; he was a warrior, a fighter. I felt his rage. Windradyne fought in the stories of backlash and of lore and of horror. Whispering their importance. *He bled for all of us mob.*

I saw Windradyne that night; he visited the polished cement freezer box where I lay. Together we looked out past the grey glue melancholy and into the diamonds in the canvas of night. He pointed up to the clustering stars and back at me. His eyes were black deep-sea pearls; he tried to say something with them. I couldn't understand

and bent my neck back up at the cradling dome. The stars scattered free and became sea birds, their wings brushing through the sky, long necks pointed upward, carving lines and unzipping the wet universe. Under its blanket was water, flowing, and blue shimmering. The water did not fall, instead it suspended.

Windradyne faded from my side and I stood lost in my thoughts as they swam through the shifting sea.

Maybe it was too much paint or too much goon. Whatever it was, Windradyne had shown me, letting me in on something important. I didn't know what it all meant. The sky showing the journey the waters make, the tracks, the beds balancing liquid from cloud to crevasse. *Follow the leatherback turtle through tide, the waterbirds fly between currents.* I knew I had to get out of the city, get out of the boxes they put you in.

The cell was silent and crying. Far off there were only hollow echoes. Morning's blue-grey light defined corners and captivity. Footsteps stalked the 'safe space' between salvation and the street.

'Wake up, on your feet, May Gibson. You

straight yet?' The uniform stood strong in the narrow corridor.

I sat upright on the metal tray and rolled the barbed blanket in my lap, bug-eyeing the sullen shadow.

'No charges this time, your four hours are up.' She passed my clothes through the metal grate. 'Get changed, get out.'

Outside the turf lapped at my feet. Suits and hand-bags began to fill the emptiness of morning. I could see Joyce's rooftop from the grass; I knew I needed to see Johnny. I knew I had to leave this place. We both did. Leave the people grieving through sleepy eyes, those only faintly dreaming. I needed to go to the water where it drew up on the riverbank and sand. I needed to listen to the dreams.

*

The front door is open; I walk inside the empty house and up the stairs. I know Johnny will be there. I know he will be waiting. Joyce is out this morning, morning tea in the elders' room at the community centre. I climb the last stairs and push open the door. Johnny sits on the edge of his bed, packing a bong.

'Hey, Wantok, thought I'd never see you again, you got caught?' He laughs his head off. 'You one of us now, May, you're a fuckin criminal like the rest of us.'

'No I'm not!'

'Yep, you are, a no-good streetie criminal!' He laughs more. 'You need to be controlled, Wantok.'

He puts the bong down and wrestles me to the bed. We're laughing.

'So whatcha doin? You going back to the squat, I don't reckon you should. Too many pigs go round there, I reckon Joyce will let ya back.' He picks the bong back up, nurses it in his hands.

'Nah, I'm leaving, I'm doing what we said we would. I'm goin to country, I'm goin to find family.'

'Yeah?' He lights the cone piece, pulls a bong.

'Yeah! Yes. *How exciting, May, that's great* – you could be at least half pissing your pants!'

'It's good, May, just miss ya, ya know.'

'Well come with me, that's why I came here, to get you, we can go the Cape and hitch in a boat or something. We can go to Waiben, find your old man. Go there first if you want and then out west or whatever. Let's just go – together. You coming?'

He licks his lips, stares at the bong and then inspects around the room full circle and back at my face. We meet eyes that know.

'I can't, Wantok. I can't go, May, they were just dreams, they still are. I got stuff to do here.'

'Like what? Get ripped?'

'Fuck off. You don't get it, you don't get that we stuck here!'

'I get that you got two legs and somewhere you want to be!'

'Nah you don't get it, that we fucking prisoners of our own prison. Gangsters Paradise, this all it is. We don't go nowhere. Just go, May.'

Near the doorway I turn around to him, pink eyed. 'You know what, Johnny; I get that you just gunna stay nobody. You ain't gunna move to change anything, not for nobody else and not even for yourself. Ever thought about it? Johnny Smith – John Smith, that's a nobody's name, you're a fuckin nobody like everyone else!'

'Yeah? That's all right with me – nobodies don't need no one either! See ya, Wantok, see ya later!'

And I leave, with our dreams spilling at our feet.

Mapping Waterglass

The coins rolled under my slipping finger-tips like greasy piano keys. It was three bucks sixty for hot chips at road stops so I had to break the twenty, which left me with more shrapnel sweating in the thrashing heat of day. Long, straight, flat, sea of black, its end a blur of hazy refuge. Caressing the road from either side, open unchanging grassland of scattered trees like bunyas. The few branches and leaves hovered over cattle, casting broken shadows that let in most of the light shine. The land a basin of scorched anguish.

A summer storm cloud swerved onto the gravel shoulder; grey dust swept across the paddock of saline orange orchards and blankets of white mini daisies. A man made up of forearms, winched himself out from the swung-open door of the ute.

'I'm heading to Wyalong, need a lift, kid?'

'Lake Cowal – goin that way?'

'Yeah, we'll get there.' He threw his stubble chin toward the passenger side. 'Get in.'

We drove the melting road for hours. Gary told me about his wife being pregnant and how happy they were, how they'd both grew up in Wyalong and left years ago only to return. Now they have a house out here and a butchery in West Wyalong that his family have run for so long that he can't remember, and how he once hitched and he knew how hard it was and he's also happy to help people out, also it makes the drive go faster, having someone to talk to and all.

'Hey, you like music?' He didn't need an answer and pushed the tape in with his fat thumb.

'Van Morrison, mate, a bloody legend.' He puffed on his belief. 'You know it?'

Pain fled from the box I stored it in. 'Brown Eyed Girl' would be my crucifix, my funeral song. Memories of my mum cruising the coast road, her thin dark forearms resting against the bus-like steering wheel, the afternoon light flashing between trees against the deep bone dents of her eye sockets. Me, riding the front seat and staring out at the wide blue ocean, shy and hoping to catch a glimpse of a whale. The humpbacks would travel up the coast to give birth and then in the summer, with their new calves, would slowly shift back down in the warmer Pacific, playing and feeding along the deep stretch from Sydney to Woonona. Mum's stories were sad, she could only whisper their importance, instead she'd show you them, take you there. She'd show you Byamee, she'd show you his work, how it was made. Whale swimming the cool currents, cursing jellyfish, still angry about losing his canoe and being tricked by the other animals. The whale had held his pain, like Mum had. And like I have.

My mum's half-decent sing-along voice bellowing through the Kombi, *you're my brown-eyed girl . . . and we used to sing.* The words were always sung like a testament to the memory, song lines to ease her absence, knowing the impermanence of our company, saying *I'm still here.*

'Yeah, I like Van Morrison, always heard it as a kid, that and Archie . . .'

His unknowing eyes smiled at me.

He lit his stories with the red brevity of match-heads. The one about his old mum who'd broken her hip a couple of years ago, never ageing as gracefully as they'd wished. The docs gave her pethidine for the pain. Pethidine to morphine, morphine to more pain, gracing her instead with addiction.

I listened as he took me to her bedside, one last tear dribbling like ripples in slow rapids over sun-burnt pastoral lines. Happy lines, sometimes sad.

He fumbled along the dash, finally spitting flint onto cigarette to mask his bloodshot eyes. He shook the pack toward me like offering black jellybeans. Our conversation gently evaporated with the smoke rings like halos over hurt. The whale held his pain, like Gary had.

'They call this place *Bland Shire* – can't half guess why.' Gary choked on his lung and laughter.

Through the sun-etched windshield, brown heritage buildings with bodgie white stone trim-mings stood like dead boab trees. Women in high-waisted stonewash jeans and tucked-in blouses gathered outside the school gates, digging their hands in tight pockets, laughing and flipping their big floppy fringes about.

'People never leave places like this, they stay the same – same neighbours, same friends, same shops, same small-town bullshit. Should change once the mine goes through, few new faces wouldn't hurt ... Lake Cowal's about twelve k's.' He spun the wheel and we kept on down the highway, watching moths meet their deathbeds against the glass. 'Give ya me number, can stay with me and me missus, we'd be happy to have ya. She cooks a bloody good roast that woman!'

The lacquer of pink sweat over his grin. He had the kindest smile I'd ever seen. I thought he could easily knock me out with his huge arms, but I knew he wouldn't.

'Yeah, thanks, see how I go, might want to stay waterfront for a while ...'

Gary interrupted my daydreams of Windradyne, pointing at the sky of dark cool water shifting across a lake, brolgas skimming along its surface, sunset, sunrise reflecting.

'You know about the mining compound, ha?'

'Nah, what?'

He nodded toward the entrance. 'You'll see.'

We pulled up in front of the barbed fence that wrapped itself around the plane of grass and small bush. Gary shone headlights on high beam against the big glossy sign.

BARRICK GOLD CANADA LTD
NOTICE OF EXPLORATION LICENCE
FOR COWAL GOLD PROJECT

'They're gunna do it, can't stop em. About three thousand hectares they're gunna dig. Gold you see, money makes the world go round, kiddo. Big guns like these guys, little guys like us, can't budge em, and not even the black fellas out there at the blockade can stop em, saying it's a sacred site and all . . . '

'Where's all the water?'

'Water!' He grunted an absurd laugh. 'Last time that *lake* had water I would have been not much older than you. There must be water somewhere under there though; otherwise they wouldn't dig, hey?'

'Yeah, thanks for the lift, Gary.'

'No worries, kiddo, you give us a phone call remember. Only a phone call away, we'll come pick ya up, ok.'

He dropped the scrunched up piece of paper and five dollars in my hand. We exchanged silent goodbyes as he slammed the gearstick into reverse and left.

The afternoon sun smothered its rays among the saltbush, honey grass danced in the skylight. A slaughter of crows and resident bats swept the expanse of sky. The crows surveyed decay. Even in the fighting city air they still bred. The bats would soon die; the crows began to nest.

Mum's stories would always come back to this place, to the lake, where all Wiradjuri would stop to drink. Footprints of your ancestors, she'd say, one day I'll take you there.

I walked around the dusty imaginary rim, dragging my fingers through the wire net. A fire was being smoked from the western side like smoke rings, halos over hurt. A large plastic banner wrapped over the path of my hand. I stepped back and watched twilight devour its paint.

Forty thousand years is a long time, forty thousand years still on my mind…

Just Dust

The church gave her the name Isabelle. Her mother gave her the name Galing, which means water dreaming. She is an elder, and that means she has a responsibility to protect what belongs to her people. To teach. She's been living at the place where they make all the white laws for the country, the Parliament House. She said all those years ago they declared an embassy, a part of government that was dedicated to her people. She lives between the embassy and this blockade at the lake where we met. Her mother's land and my mother's land.

The mining company want to leach cyanide underneath the saltbush land. Issy says that they make a blockade and stay there for as long as it takes for them company shareholders to back out, for company to leave, take their fences, their electricity, take all their machines and generators and leave. Take themselves and don't come back.

Issy says they don't understand that just because you can't see something, don't mean it's not there. She says that under the earth, the land we stand on, under all this there is water. She's says that our people are born from quartz crystal, hard water. We are powerful people, strong people. Water people, people of the rivers and the lakes.

They look at the land and say there is nothing here.

wiray – no

dhuray – having

We laugh at that, it is our little joke.

Because we've got plenty, she says, smiling.

Issy smooths her wiry hair with an open palm, gently. Hair the colour of ash, and under the gaze of flames she seems alight. Her face is a pool of small pulses, bumps and folds, lines taking us which ways. Her eyes are small slivers and they shine like fish scales. They are lucid and kind, but almost feverish as she speaks.

Issy says that the lake works like a heart, pumping its lifeblood from under the skin. She says there are many hearts, and with them, many valves and veins. This, she adds, as smoke dances across her shadowy lips, is all life. *murun*. Everything is part of the heart, everything is water, and when we listen closely we can hear the shifting beneath us, the gathering above us, and within us a churning.

She says that they want to dig up the hearts, free out the veins, dam up the valves so they can live. Hungrily. With gold and steel towers. She says they are building high to get closer to father sky, closer to heaven. It doesn't work, she grins, and they will always fall. The jewels will go back to the mother eventually.

She takes a saltbush branch from the coals and draws a circle in the dust.

Issy says that everything is sacred, inside the circle and outside the circle; she says that we should look after both areas the same. They are magic, she adds.

She takes the branch again and outlines the circle twice, each circle a little bigger than the other, and then she draws smaller circles from the first circle inwards. She makes another circle the same, next to it and joins the two with a short line. She says that we need to come back. Listen.

What are the other lines, I ask?

She smooths her hair again, pursing her mouth knowingly, and watches the light undo between us.

You want to find the Gibsons, you say? Then you will follow the Lachlan, tomorrow, follow Bila snake to Euabalong.

She gets up to leave.

What about this, I ask. Pointing at the snaking canvas.

That's just dust isn't it.

What are the lines?

Just dust too isn't it.

Cocoon

We're sitting around the pit in the backyard, the fire burning our shins and toes. Baking taut red skin. Mum pulls in from the beach on the bike, her boney fingers steering up the side of the house and into the orange backlight. Her crazy hair entangled in the branch's twig arms. As she leans the bike down she trips a little over her sandshoes and gathers the kindling again under her elbow. I notice for maybe the first time that she is so old, my mother, but she's still so young. A plastic bag stretches with a West Coast Cooler at the side of her thigh.

I loved fire nights. Most nights. We had a permanent fire pit, Billy and me dug out sandstone rocks and put them around the edge for sitting. Mum liked sitting on them, hanging her upper body over her knees, pulling out clumps of grass and melting them against the hot coals. When she'd be telling us stories she'd carve out little lizards and lotus flowers and fish shapes in the rock stools. They were so pretty. I liked sitting on the grass, getting as close as I could to the flame. Billy would crouch at the fire, one leg bent under his bum and the other tucked in, his chin resting on his knee. He'd break the kindling with his hands, or if the branch was too thick he'd flop up and slam his shoe into its diagonal. His hair flinging as he snapped it into halves.

He'd show us how to feed the fire, making sure it never went out. My brother was so good with the fire, a delicate drop or nudge of each stick. He'd blow and talk to the coals, mumble at them, building a high tepee. Fussing over it, prodding and poking and caressing its belly. He'd sit back on his ankles and bend his elbows onto a sandstone rock, laying his body out across the side of the fire. Sometimes Mum would have a West Coast Cooler, I'd watch the white fizzing sneeze hiss and disappear in the warm air. Take a sip, ahhhhhh. Better.

The flames would lap at Billy dangling his fingertips over the fire. Mum warning. The night always stealing us, into twirling smoke and constellations. Waiting for Mum to forget that it's a school night and be able to rave on about the days under the sun. We'd try to distract her all night, so she'd forget, ask her to tell us more stories, on and on until she'd start to doze off in the warm womb of the fire.

They were the best times, the three of us at the fire, laughing and talking over the top of the things we never talked about. Like that sad in her eyes or Billy's or mine. It was kind of funny, making everything seem more important than our hearts. But I suppose it *was* then. We were only kids anyway, nothing had affected us yet. It seemed like the only time Billy would talk, lots anyway.

I remember him being so excited about the canoe that he'd found in someone's footpath garbage collection once. He told us about dragging it across the lawns and having to lift the thing on his back when he came to a crossing. Him being so careful not to shatter the fibreglass shell. Billy talked about sanding it down and making a trailer for it out of our old bike wheels, so he could tow it to the beach and I remember him telling Mum about how he could go canoeing in the ocean and catch snapper for dinner. He talked all that night about the canoe, and every night for weeks about how the trailer was coming along, and then eventually about his trips off the shore, how scary it was, but fun. All the awesome creatures he met below.

I remember he came back one afternoon, just past twilight, when the waves start to grey and blur. Mum had just got the firewood together when Billy cruised through the side gates, big grin on his face and a big fish in his fist, holding it by the tail. Mum was so proud, I remember, patting Billy on the back and shy laughing.

We cooked the snapper on the fire that night, fried on a skillet. It was the best night, just before Mum left us. Billy telling us about the brush with the big fish, how he saw humpbacks heading up the coast, sending the fish toward the canoe, about netting it up real easy. About the ocean, about the gifts, how happy he was. How happy he was. And I knew it too, he was. We were.

Bíla Snake

The river sleeps, nascent of limpid green, tree bones of spirit people, arms stretched out and screaming. And at their fingertips claws of blue bonnets, sulphur-crested cockatoos and the erratic dips and weaves of wild galahs, grapefruit pink and ghost grey splash the sky. And as the salt subsides, the green trickles over the riverbank from tree limbs, spilling colour into day's light, upside down. The water moves in tiptoes, and you could almost mistake it for a painting, staining only the top edge of the bank with its stirring: red orange ochre to cherry blood. This dust, this bleeding ash, is everywhere.

One of her arms rests at the small of her back, the other hangs at her empty hip. It waits until something moves, or for a word to jump at her finger. Issy points, *budyaan . . . muraany . . .*

budyabudya. Bird . . . cockatoo . . . butterfly. She laughs, eyes wide. *Bila,* river.

She tells me to follow for four days the left side of the river, only cross once at the *cuundabul-len* – where the water shallows. I should cross to get onto the road, walk for a few hundred metres to get food, and then walk back to the river. I ask her how I will know that I'm there. She says there is a tourist sign, big blue and yellow one, of a knife and a plate and a fork, to show me. We laugh. She says I might die from starvation, but probably not. 'Plenty of fish if you can catch em,' she adds. 'You'll be all right, cook up a feed with those ciggies you got, make a little fire.'

She waves her hands together to create a pile of cigarettes in our talking. Here at the water, away from the blockade and the sad fire, she is light and spilling laughter at my foolishness. But under all the giggling we meet somewhere between my blazing stomach and the stars, and she looks into me with a gravity. I think of it as a shared stubbornness or some nature of knowing. It leaks from her, that once she too was lost.

She enfolds her lined hands again and places one palm on her chest and the other on her waistband. 'Listen.' The word overflows the bird noise and echoing doubt. 'Nganhali ngalang-ganha bubay bargan.' She smiles and knots her hands again behind her. She shuffles her skinny legs toward the road. Turns back to me. 'Bargan is boomerang,' she smiles again. 'You'll be back.'

I close my eyes. When I open them she is gone.

And I begin. One foot in front of another and so on.

I remember what my mum had said to me once about worries. She said when we worry, when something is pulling us down, we should take a walk. A good walk, she said, a long walk. Rhythm tangles behind you, scurries up ahead, and somehow in between, something makes sense. One foot is your heart and one foot is your mind. Together, they can make your worries easy, clearer. 'Just walk,' she'd say, 'just gotta walk.'

I suppose in the end she couldn't find her feet.

And with the crying inside me, that I could not make out, of words or voice, I began to walk.

Listen, Issy had said.

I listened. And the voices would come out,

emerging from button grasses, bark shavings and water. Mother. Brother. Anger. Fear. All soaked in sorrow. Intricate words like Joyce's photo tree of faces. Day doused them yellow, but night crawled the dark moons, hiding light. And answers.

Each day I asked the voices, why I'm here? What I'm doing?

They did not answer. But I kept asking anyway, to make sure that it was ok. Still they did not tell.

Hours edged by like the river reeds, drifting and poisonous. I caught an old slow carp with my jumper, tied at its end, swimming like an air balloon in the eddy. It was a crazy plan, but I was lucky. I longed for the beach where in the shallows we would always find pipis. I burnt the stupid fish and swore at the river that second night. I was so mad, not at the fish or the river or the lonely path I was prodding, but at that bickering in my head. The noisy silence, it itched my skin.

The next morning, dodging pipes that drank from the river to sprinklers, was the big tourist sign on the side of the bridge. There was the table setting, yellow on blue. CONDOBOLIN – THE LACHLAN VALLEY WAY.

I followed the edge of the empty highway to the little town and bought a hamburger, eating the last of the money with the hope of a family dinner. I knew my mother's mob would give me a feed, when I got there – to Euabalong – when I found them anyway. I dribbled beetroot and lettuce water down my forearms and onto the footpath, imagining these people. I imagined my mum would be there too, they'd all be there, around a fire, cooking goanna. I imagined them whispering the stories my mum had whispered years ago, singing with the firelight licking their head-dresses, matching my odd looking eyes with theirs. Peeling back my skin, my blood against theirs. Family. My people. My mob.

Yamakarra, I would say. I practised it as I walked the rest of the river.

Yamakarra, they would say.

Mission

The buckles of the seat belts stabbed into my hips from either side. We rocked against each other's hot brown skin, arms and shoulders colliding as the car bulleted through road ditches. The heat slashed open the tar, burning and thrashing at the Commodore's yellow bonnet, sending daggers of white light into our eyes. Choking, dirty ciggie smoke and ash swelled the back seat, where we rode. It carved out a queasy feeling in my hunger stomach. My feet scrambled atop, sliding empties on the floor that exhaled their stale beer smell.

'Thanks for the ride,' I said as I stepped out onto the red dirt.

'No worries.'

The mission is the outpost between two towns, Euabalong, where I'd come from and Lake Cargelligo, where they were going. When

I got from the river to Euabalong I asked at the general store where I'd find family. Go to the mission, they said, where the highway crossed. They'd know where your family is, they said.

From the side of the highway the land seemed lathed bare. I couldn't imagine anyone living there. I spun around a few times and dizzied over the starkness, a tiny arrow-shaped sign blinked in the distance, black on white. 'Mission', it read.

I wandered over and looked down the rusty track to its petrol-fumed end. I should be used to it by now, walking, but hope was becoming weary. I could think only about food, my shadow stretched out like a rake along the track. When the dirt turned to bitumen houses began to line the emptiness of daylight. Sadness clawed into my skin for no reason I could see. Everything – houses, sealed road, gutter, sports oval – seemed normal. I supposed they rose up like the estate homes, from the flat bare ground, a hasty construction of identical walls, devoid of emotion, shuffled off to the new suburb like secrets in pockets. Not to make too much noise, not to draw too much attention, not to fuss.

So you have to look closer.

Bare red ground sweeps all distance. Little pockets of black-green trees remain still and burning. To the south an offshoot of the Lachlan is almost dried up. There are water tanks instead. Dead land. Crops seem more important than people, than rape. A small church flakes off its old salmon skin, revealing the ashen wood beneath. The windows have no shutters, some doorways have no doors, and every house is exactly the same, like someone's idea of fancy concentration camps. People spill in and out of their houses, trying to find some kind of un-itchy medium, trying to prise off the boundaries. Kids run the streets, owning them. The sports field looks more like a rodeo pit, the last slip of the green cricket pitch is beginning to brown, like everything else. It feels forgotten here, and if you can forget about a place so forgettable, so unassuming, then I imagine the people who live in it forget too. Forget that there exist places beyond the highway creases, forget that someone might care.

'Hey! Excuse me! Young lady, get ere.'

He waves me over to his seat on the back porch. The old man is so black, the blackest skin I'd ever seen. He wears a worn-out cowboy shirt and a big Akubra hat, black jeans, bare feet. The line of shade from the rooftop cuts off at his face. He points me over to sit on the other side, in the rest of the shade; a half case of throwdowns sits between us. He twists over so we face each other.

'I sit half in the shade and half in the sun. That's because,' he pauses and raises a long finger to the sky, 'if ya get too used to the shade ya don't ever want to get up. And I don't want to get used to anything, ha!'

He strikes his finger into the air, as if to burst a bubble and laughs. 'My name is Graham, but I'm Uncle to ya young fellas.' We nod together. 'What ya doin here anyway, young lady, not Christian are ya?'

'Nah, I'm not Christian, why?'

'Let us have a few more of these before I start on about all that, ha!'

He tosses his fist of VB in the air; it flips across the lawn, and rests against the fence. He cracks another.

'So you from lake there or what?'

'Nah, I just come from Sydney, Uncle.'

'Oh, the big smoke? True? That's deadly girl, I

like it there, people so wired up, things to do. Not like dis place! What you come ere for then, all the way from city?'

'For family, trying to find my family.'

'What they name?'

'Gibson.'

'Mmm, I know some Gibsons in Cowra, bit far from here though. Gibson spose to be a big deadly mob, strong people you know! Where they spose to be?'

'Euabalong, but there's none there, they said to come here.'

'True, someone will know, maybe old Betty, but she's in town, she'll be back soon, we'll ask her, ok?'

I nod.

'See that house there, that where she live, we see her come back, ok?'

I nod again. 'Ok,' I say.

'Betty's a good lady, she one of the only old ones here that knows what's what, she got trouble though, all her boys too much on the grog, and her husband too, too much grog and bustin each other up, ya know. It's no good, this entire place is gone, no spirit left here. Only bad spirits come to wake em up, ya see em at the river there, three very tall dark men, so tall, with red eyes like desert peas. They come to wake people up, but you never look in the eyes, cos when you do, you become them. Bad spirit. Nobody go to the river no more. Got good and got bad, always two sides. Poor old people ere got round up ere from the tank, where lots of our people were killed from them sickness, that's these people, Wiradjuri and my people – Nygampaa. Back in '47 government made this place and shifted plenty of station blacks out ere, that's what they call us, station blacks. Bloody Catholics run the places, bloody run places into the ground. You know some of our people, they been taken into the church and them priests have their way, ya know bad spirit in them, and they took it out on the little fellas. Who's gunna speak up for em little fellas? Other people don't understand, when that bad spirit happens to family, it stays in the family, when we born we got all our past people's pain too. It doesn't just go away like they think it does.'

He paused his story, took the last of the throw-down into his mouth. 'That's why so much drinkin, drinkin, drinkin. That's why so much anger, you know? You musta see it in Sydney there; ya know what I'm talkin about. Well then these people never get to talk and it builds up inside em, it just want to get out and when it does it destroy em and they get locked up in the prisons with all that pain they gotta listen to, alone in they prisons, all the memories chokin em in they sleep. No one to talk about it, no one ever want to talk about it. And they die, kill em selves, then those governments just put another number, nother cross on they list. Lockin up bloody young fellas, why we have prisons? So they don't have to think about it, about people's problems, we don't have to do anything bout it. They still tryin to do it, kill off us fellas, that always been they plan, now they do it quiet, crush em, slow. Ya see the problem is, us fellas still seen as second-rate person, still treated like they don't matter. Bloody millennium come and gone and they still can't treat our people right. We seen forty bloody millenniums, our people, and they government give us credit for that? Only when it suits them, when they gotta show all them tourists. This country, this government and them bad churches, they all one evil, ya know, they all workin with each other. You probably sitting ere thinkin I'm

just crazy old jackeroo, don't know what I'm talkin
bout! You know what, maybe I don't know what
I'm talkin bout, I sure as hell would like someone
to tell me I'm wrong. I wish someone would just
tell me I'm wrong.

'See dat, there Betty comin, go an catch her.'

He points across the road at the car pulling in
to the driveway.

I jump up and grab my bag. 'Thank you,
Uncle.'

'That's ok, girl, go on, go ask for your family,
ya find em.'

I turn and start running across the lawn,
'Hey, young lady, take your hat off for old Betty,
ok?'

'Ok.'

I run across to the cement drive and slow
down as I near the people grabbing groceries
from the car boot. An older woman notices me. I
know it's Betty. I take off my hat. We say hello as
we nod to each other.

'My name is May Gibson; I'm looking for
some of my family, the Gibsons?'

Betty cradles the bag of packet food between
us as the younger men slink past carrying slabs of

beer under their arms. 'Gibson. You know Lake Cargelligo?'

'No.'

She turns to the skinny woman in the car, telling her the street name. The woman nods.

'My daughter Jo, she take you there, the only Gibsons left I reckon, love. Quick jump in!'

The engine kicks over and Betty waves to us both, a trying smile on her face and soft eyes that turn away as we leave. Seemed all so perfect, so right.

Country

The house is white. It sits on the square of ruby sand and clipped grass, a few metres back from the short fishnet fence and the camellia bed. A narrow path creases from the gate to the peppermint door, which is shaded by a candy stripe awning. The street smells of mothballs and farming. This, they say, is the Gibson house, the only Gibsons left.

My knuckles rub at the mesh of the screen door. I know I should knock, but my hand is scared. This is not how it is supposed to be.

Inside the house is quiet. A dog is barking from one of the yards. I move my fist across to the doorframe. I knock. A woman comes to the doorway; she has a glass in her hand, lemon lime, a cigarette cropped from her finger's edge.

'Hello there?'

'Hello, I'm looking for the Gibsons.'

'Yes, that's me, me and my husband, who are you, love?'

'May Gibson.'

'Hold on, I'll get the keys.'

She comes back to the screen, snips the lock, tumbling the keys, and opens the sketched wire onto our difference.

We see our difference.

'Percy. Percy love, come here.' Her eyes stray over her shoulder. 'Hold on a minute.'

She disappears and I want to get out of there.

It's too late; he is here under the candy aluminium awning. The spitting image of Mum. All skin and hard face.

'Who are your parents?'

'June Gibson's my mum.'

'June, little June, last time I saw June, she would have been this tall.' He points a cigarette to her height above the ground.

'Come in, come in . . . May isn't it?'

'Yep.'

'Dotty, Dotty, this is May, my . . . well I suppose, well I don't know who you'd be to me . . . June's mother was my aunt, so spose you're my cousin too or something.'

He scratches his head, dropping ash onto the thick milky carpet as he lowers his cigarette out toward the chair. 'Sit, sit. You want some cordial, May?'

'Yeah, thanks.'

'Well, little June, hey, ahh jeez . . . where is she now?'

'She's gone . . . I mean, she's dead.'

'Ahh shit, how long.'

'Six years.'

'It's funny when you said gone I thought ya meant walkin, you know travellin, cos her mother, Alice, your grandmother, my aunty, she was a gypsy, all your Gibson family, lots of gypsies.'

'Spose you're gypsy too, ha?' He looks at my small backpack and down at my feet. His lip crawls cruelly. 'What d'ya want anyway love, ya come here for money, ha? Like your grandmother?'

'No.'

'No? Well what ya come here for? Where'd ya come from anyway?' His voice is louder and intruding.

'Wollongong, sort of. I came here, well I don't know really, not for friggin money though!'

'Gotta a bit cheek too, ha?'

'I'm not the person you're lookin at me like, I'm not a criminal.'

'Never said you were, love. Not for money, ha? I believe ya. Spit it out then, I got golf in a minute.'

'Just wanted to know about my family, you know, the Gibsons, where they come from and stuff. My mum, she told me loads of stories and stuff and I just was expecting to find, I dunno, some family or something . . . '

'Stories, ha! What do you want to know? Where ya get ya skin from, ya tribal name, ya totem, ya star chart, the meaning of the world? Thought us Gibsons'd give ya the answers, ha!'

I back toward the door.

'Nah nah, look here.' He waves me back to sit. 'Look.'

He balances the meeting out on his knees, asking his hands for words.

I interrupt the silence. 'It's all right, I'll just go, sorry.'

'Nah nah, listen, sit down.'

'Your grandmother she left this place, went looking for something, some kind of meaning, something that wasn't the mission, or the tank, or the farming or something. She came back here once, thirty years later, my father, her brother, didn't even recognise her at first, standing on the porch with a bunch of kids hanging off her hands. Your mother, she was one of them. She wanted money. I remember she was desperate, sad. Some drover, white fella, name of Jack or something or other had messed her around. We gave her some money, and a feed and a bed. And then she took the kids with her and left. That was it.'

My thoughts drifted off to Mum, when she was going crazy, telling us about a man called Jack, I remember she used to say he was the first white man to destroy us. 'Not the last,' she would say, stuck on the words. 'Not the last.'

I wanted to be free of them – I wanted pride instead.

'What about like, growing up here, like learning from your old people and stuff?'

'You're just like your grandmother, you know that? But she knew it. She died of hope, you know that? The thing is, we weren't allowed to be what you're looking for, and we weren't told what was right, we weren't taught by anyone. There is a big missing hole between this place and the place you're looking for. That place, that people, that something you're looking for. It's gone. It was taken away. We weren't told, love; *we weren't allowed to be Aboriginal.*

'I got a good life now.' He nods at the TV, hiding welled eyes, and then at the furniture, the thick carpet, Dotty sitting at the table, smoking. 'Stories, ha! Your mother probably read em from books, plenty of books if ya want to learn.' He shakes his head at his knees, huffs and lifts himself off the armchair. He makes a point of looking at his wristwatch. 'I got to go to golf now, nice to meet you, May. Dotty will make you something to eat if you want.'

I do not cry, my eyes are hardened, like honey-comb, like toffee. Brittle, crumbling sugar. He puts his hand out toward me; we shake hands, a pact that I won't be here digging up his past when he gets back.

And I'm not.

*

The highway breeze is thick and hot from the truck's cab. Earth spins up in little tornadoes over bare grazing fields, clouds tumble from the east into purple storm, the birds leave for cover, their wings gracing wind. And day leads night, headlights stretch over the glass, and pass. Eventually I will be there. At the shoreline, we need to talk.

And it all makes sense to me now. Issy's drawing in the sand, boundaries between the land and the water, *us*, we come from the sky and the earth and we go back to the sky and the earth, bone and fluid. This land *is* belonging, all of it for all of us. This river is that ocean, these clouds are that lake, these tears are not only my own. They belong to the whales, to Joyce; they belong to Charlie, to Gary, to Johnny, to Issy, to Percy, to Billy, to Aunty, to my nannas, to their nannas, to their great nannas' neighbours. They belong to the spirits. To people I will never even know. I give them to my mother.

The driver says he's going for a shower and said we'll be back on the road straight after. He pulls the big trailer into the truckstop. I swing down out of the cab and close the door above my head. In the service station I walk the chip aisles, bringing back flashes of Cheapa Petrol and then of the Block – of that big place of family, Joyce, Johnny, everyone.

I scan the pretty white faces on the magazine covers, and down to the stacks of newspapers that I'd never read. And then, it was as if my world slipped through the hands I'd only just found. The newspaper broke the news, as hard and as real as it needed to be. BOY, 16, DIES IN POLICE CHASE. The photo of Johnny was magic, one of old Joyce's off the wall. He had the biggest grin spilling across his face, his Wu-Tang hat hiding all the beautiful dreaming in his head.

I couldn't cry for Johnny now. I'd only be crying for the harsh words that I'd said when I left. He died at least with that perfect dream, that perfect paradise, that perfect Thursday Island in his mind. He could go fishing now, cruising the strait, like Mungi, I thought – *peacefully forever*, over our crumbling skin, through this shifting water.

The Jacaranda Tree

I have jagged recollections. Sharp paper clippings that I remember. I could burrow into another time, or by chance be harked back, and I would stand in our old backyard searching the fence line, naming the things that remain, in the nook of my head. Against the fence I could trace back to someone's face, their mouth, their eye socket, their ear. I tried so many times to find my mother's, but I could only pretend to recognise her, her real face is lost.

And I would come to the jacaranda tree, its dogwood trunk writhing through the palings. Heaving in all its purple-belled loveliness. My eyes would find first its feet, entangled roots rigging from fence poles underfoot. Sometimes the other trees' roots would be so invading that they would splinter plumbing, unbloating reservoir. Though the jacaranda shared its ground.

The lean body of the trunk breached over the backyard. Fishbone fern leaves like tinselled brush, rows of ordered confetti concealing its embryo limbs within. Its milky coffee skin. After summer the tiny leaves would be washed in mustard through the wind and fall, back to the earth, feeding its roots, and that entire hidden body would be exposed. It stayed naked for a lot of the year, until I only remembered its familiar bareness. Then one day, maybe home from school, or early in the morning peering at the tilting sun and cloud stream, there would be a single tiny green bulbus, with the smallest speck of mauve at its end. Bubblegum dipped.

It was a sneaky arrival, never witnessed, a wondrous secretive thing. And then day by day, as if the beans had spilt and the tree had nothing left to hide, handfuls of clustered trumpets dressed its boughs. As more purple emerged in the deeper spring, others would ballet downward to the grass. I would scoop up armfuls and scatter the bells over my bed, their wet collapsing petals blotting blankets and carpet. And then there would be none, no evidence of its beauty, only the watery stains of a visit. And later the entire cycle would enfold again, a slow gentle process, like the wearing out of shoe soles.

One year, in the jacaranda's bleakness Mum had strung a tyre-swing onto its fattest branch. I remember swinging from its rubber ring a few times, sort of rocking slightly back and forth. She took it back down the following year, revealing a bruise-worn elbow where the tree-swing roped its wing. We decided to let the jacaranda be, and marvelled from the back door or the grass instead. Too delicate to be touched.

It's a sacred bloody pest. It isn't meant to be here, I hate it, too pretty, she'd say, threatening always to chop it down. Though I once found her eyes glue and she almost smiled at its gifts, a bouquet of blue jays, the most beautiful thing in the entire street.

It's an odd thing, a backyard, a little strip of nature, a little reminder of the rest of it, elsewhere. A little piece of earth – a garden, a few trees, a clothesline and a fire pit maybe. Somewhere for the sun to hide.

It was summer when she went away, early December I think. The jacaranda would've still been in bloom, toward the end of a cycle. And they say that they found her there, lying under that pest of a tree. I imagine she made peace with it then, or just gave in. I imagine her among the spread of purple. Jacaranda petals and blood, softened and returned.

How quiet it would've been, how beautiful.

Home

The moon tows the tide in and out twice a day forever. When I come home the tide is flowing in, when I reach it, when it draws in across the purple slate beds of the point, through the rain and across the grit sand, soaking under my feet, salt bubbles burst at my shins. Then, I know that I am home.

We don't need words. I can smell it. I can feel it. The raindrops are gentle and cold, the beach is empty, only the salt smell of the ocean air and freshwater clouds fill the space. The wind is blowing nor-easterly, yellow and red flags flutter further down the beach, huddling no one into the safety. Gulls cruise the air, scanning the shoreline and dunes; I'm not sure what they're looking for. They have waterproof feathers, I imagine. I pull my hood down over my face.

The ocean is sad grey, except in the shallows

where the water is pearl and when a wave peels up you can catch the beautiful jade flashing milky through the lips. A secret. The shore-breakers tumble up the banks, tossing sand through their whitewash waves. The headland is foggy in the distance. Behind me, the escarpment is just a flat silhouette.

As I walk up toward the beach entrance, across the little raindrop dimples on yesterday's footprints, and feel the gritty warm-wet sand carry me. As the starburst eelgrass clusters roll like tumbleweeds off the dunes. As all the salt hits me. I know what the word really means, home.

My mother knows that I am home, at the water I am always home. Aunty and my brother, we are from the same people, we are of the Wiradjuri nation, *hard water*. We are of the river country, and we have flowed down the rivers to estuaries to oceans. To live by another stretch of water. Salt.

Even though this country is not my mother's country, even though we are freshwater, not saltwater people, this place still owns us, still owns our history, my brother's and my own, Aunty's too. Mum's. They are part of this place; I know now that I need to find them.

I could run away again, I could run away from the pain my family holds. I could take the yarndi, the paint, the poppies, and all the grog in the world but I couldn't run from the pain and I couldn't run from my family either.

When Billy and me lost our mother, we lost ourselves. We stopped swimming in the ocean, scared that we'd forget to breathe. Forget to come up for mouthfuls of air. We lost trust because we didn't want to touch something that was going to fall away. Like bubbles, too delicate, too fragile, too brief.

*

When I get there, Paradise Parade is warring. Walls compress into the ground, rooftops twist over levelled clay, fences warn me off, pipes penetrate cement blocks, toilets sit beside sinks in the air. Yellow machines have paused for a while, waiting for the cloud sky to give way. Few houses remain. The crows begin to nest.

'When ya gunna get this fuckin fence fixed, Aunty?'

I holler into the back window as I slip through the broken palings, laughing. I jump the stairs in one leap and enter the back door. Aunty leans against the cupboards, pouring a longneck into a glass. She sees me, and she sees the beer that she's holding in her shaky hand. Her back hits the cupboard doors and she slides down onto the lino, the bottle drops, and beer swims and soaks into the peepholes in the floorboards.

Aunty is crying, I cannot stop her crying.

'It's all right, Aunty, sit up, sit up.'

Billy comes out of the lounge room, leans down and hooks his arm under her shoulder.

'May, wherev you been?' Aunty sobs. 'Oh girl, I'm gone, movin' out, they kicking me out.'

Billy holds out a bucket of his arms for her wet face. He looks up at me. He's back, all eyes and face. I can tell he's clean. My brother smiles.

Aunty is crying. I cannot stop her crying.

The house, even through wall plaster that crumbles with the absence, is still home. I sit at the kitchen table. It feels good; it feels right for the first time in a long time to be home. The table still parades its paradise years; I flick my thumb through the changes, tablecloth over tablecloth. I count a dozen or so, some stuck to each other, some rotting. Soft felt, crumpled mouldy lace, linen and sticky stiff plastic. I remember coming to visit with Mum on the times when Aunty'd bought a new tablecloth. It was almost exciting, just watching her pull it out of the shopping bag, unwrap its packaging, shaking it out in the kitchen, the smell of raw plastic. Flowers. Fish. Stars. And still, a country paddock of everlastings print the tabletop, wine and fallen ashtray stains. The same as when I'd left.

'Let's go buy a new tablecloth, Aunty!'

Billy shifts his eyes from my hand as he speaks. Aunty looks at him, a bundle of pickled skin in his arms, she looks at me. Smiles.

'Yeah? A nice new one, eh?'

'Yeah, Aunty, an orange one,' I add.

'A bright fuckin orange one!' she yells and slaps her palm against the floor, laughing.

'That'll show em lovies, Aunty ain't goin any-where! Not with a tablecloth to wear in!'

She laughs excitedly, but it is too much. The water rises and cries.

I look out the window, toward the gulls div-ing between the air currents. They dance. The clouds give way to the sky, the wind has changed its course and from here the ocean is clear, waves peel across the glass, clean and hollow, spray dances off their paring lips. Falling silver rains on the afternoon bluegum sheet. The water rises and cries.

Specks of black wet-suited bodies paddle, gliding toward the next set. They always go for the second wave, the second wave of the set, swarming for that ride, to stand for as long as possible.

An excavator starts its smothering engine over the torrent of each barrel. Over the sun. Over the blue. And I wonder, if we stand here, if we stay, if they stop digging up Aunty's backyard, stop digging up a mother's memory, stop digging up our people, maybe then, we'll all stop crying.

Acknowledgments

Thank you, Sue Abbey, a wonderful editor and a beautiful friend; Madonna Duffy and UQP for being more than just publishers; Janet Hutchinson for pulling everything together; Peter Bishop and Varuna – The Writers House.

Much respect to Frank Moorhouse, Steve Kinnane, Fiona Doyle, Sam Wagan Watson, Nick Earls, John Harms, Dan Kelly, Larissa Behrendt, Judy Atkinson and Mick Martin for inspiring wisdom and encouragement.

Thanks to Reon and the Fisher family, Jenny, Nick, Michele, Cristen, Melody, Trent, Mark and Sam and Tina, Eliza, Simon Mumme, Luke Beasley, Dave Lavercombe, Patty, Owen, Courtney, Shannon blakboy, Shane and Jeremy for giving constant time, love, patience and laughter.

And thank you to my family, Mum, Dad, Tania, Billy and Andrew, Brenda and Mick, Nana and Pop.

Other Black Australian Writing from UQP

HER SISTER'S EYE
Vivienne Cleven

'. . . always remember where you're from . . .'

To the Aboriginal families of Mundra this saying brings either comfort or pain. To Nana Vida it is what binds the generations. To the unwilling savant Archie Corella it portends a fate too cruel to name. For Sophie Salte, whose woman's body and child's mind make her easy prey, nothing matters while her sister Murilla is there to watch over her.

For Murilla, fierce protector and unlikely friend to Caroline Drysdale, wife of the town patriarch, what matters is survival. In a town with a history of vigilante raids, missing persons and unsolved murders, survival can be all that matters.

The stories – of the camp, the boy and his snake, the shooting – told and passed on, offer a release from the horrors of our past. As Nana Vida says, *'That's the story. I let it go now.'*

'This is a brilliant literary novel that leaves you with a resonance of sadness long after you finish reading.'
Australian Bookseller & Publisher

ISBN 0 7022 3283 1

HOME
Larissa Behrendt

Winner of the 2002 David Unaipon Award for Indigenous Writers

Home is a powerful novel from an author who understands both the capacity of language to suppress and the restorative potency of stories that bridge the past and present. Young lawyer Candice sets out on her first visit to her ancestral homeland. When she arrives at the place where her grandmother was abducted in 1918, her family's story begins to unfold and Candice discovers the consequences of dark skin and the relentless pull of home.

> 'A stunning first novel. Behrendt creates vivid characters whose convincing inner lives bring this story of loss and survival powerfully to life.'
>
> Kate Grenville

> 'This novel's greatest strength is its insight into the pain and inherited shame of being a racist society.'
>
> *Sydney Morning Herald*

> 'Behrendt brilliantly explores the subtleties of race and identity in a palpable way. It is like getting under another's skin.'
>
> *The Age*

ISBN 0 7022 3407 9